MIXED PATHS

MIXED PATHS

YOUTH WRITERS CHALLENGE SERIES, VOL 3

Camille Carmichael, Dream Ford, Kayla Mason, Kendall Jackson, and Preston Staten Hall

MIXED PATHS

Published by Publish Your Gift®
An imprint of Purposely Created Publishing Group, LLC

Printed in the United States of America

ISBN: 978-1-64484-639-1 (print)
ISBN: 978-1-64484-638-4 (ebook)

Special discounts are available on bulk quantity purchases by book clubs, associations and special interest groups. For details email: sales@publishyourgift.com or call (888) 949-6228.
For information logon to: www.PublishYourGift.com

AUTHORS

Camille Carmichael

Dream Ford

Kayla Mason

Kendall Jackson

Preston Staten Hall

*Thank you to everyone who has supported
the Youth Writer Challenge, Inc. and
the Youth Writers Rock organizations.*

*Thank you to the instructors who helped this project:
Patricia Johnson-Harris, Roger Harris,
Deborah Billips, Jackie J.C. Gardner, and
Jackie Anderson*

TABLE OF CONTENTS

PREFACE

Welcome to "Mixed Paths," a story that is told from different perspectives. There are two sides to every story, and then there is the truth somewhere in between. The characters speak to the reader from their points of view, and although fictional, you will see much of their story in real-life situations that are relatable to young and old alike.

This story's main characters, Caniya and Karden, embark on an unexpected journey. In life, sometimes we're on the right path. Then there are times our paths are chosen for us and other times where we choose the wrong path. But every now and then, as Caniya and Karden will find out, paths can cross in unexpected ways. There's no telling what's on the other side, but you have to keep pushing forward, even if your paths are mixed with sunshine and rain.

There are always lessons along the way, and the two BFFs are about to find out that their chosen paths will have surprising outcomes that will change their lives forever.

Chapter 1
THE FASHION DESIGNER – CANIYA

Dream Ford

"I'm *done!*" sixteen-year-old Caniya said after a mother-daughter talk turned ugly. She continued saying to herself, "I can't believe she just walked out of my room and slammed my bedroom door." Caniya was frantically walking around her room in circles trying to make sense of the mean and ugly things that had been said.

"Oh, she has no idea what she has started. But I'm about to end it." Caniya threw three pairs of jeans into a small suitcase. With anger in her voice, she started rambling under her breath, confessing her frustrations about her mom.

School had ended only a few days ago, and already, the Florida sun was hot enough to fry eggs on the sidewalk. Caniya was looking forward to a great summer with no drama, but her mother wasn't about to let that happen.

Caniya, still in her feelings, vented, "She's just jealous 'cause I've got talent. She always wanted to work in fashion, but it's not my fault she decided to have two more kids and a whole husband." Then she tossed a few more items into the suitcase—tops, PJs, sneakers, leggings, and whatever else she thought necessary to leave for several days.

Caniya continued ranting. "I'm going to prove to her that I can make it without her support. I'm not taking this anymore. She is getting on my nerves. She really doesn't love me the way she loves my little sister, Isis, and my younger brother, Cole. I'll show her! She will see that I've got what it takes to be a fashion designer and model!"

This gigantic blowup had Caniya's head pounding, and her heart started racing just thinking about how disrespectful and goofy her mother was acting.

Where would I be if my real dad was still in my life? was just one of the thoughts swirling around in her head. Recalling all her mom's harsh words was having a negative impact on her, and her head felt as if it might explode.

She lay back on her bed, hoping that being still would help it to stop, but instead, the bed started spinning like a scene straight out of *The Wizard of Oz*. She could feel her body stiffening up and becoming tense, so Caniya shut her eyes, pressed her arms close to her side, and pushed the palms of her hands against the bed and repeatedly told herself to relax. Then she began to hum a tune that was soothing to her mind and body.

As her headache eased, she encountered a feeling of weightlessness like she was floating on a fluffy white cloud high in the sky. Caniya had fallen into a deep sleep for about thirty minutes, which activated a chain of dreams.

First, she envisioned her parents fussing. It was a flashback of her mother, Sheila, and her father, Richard, arguing in their bedroom. Caniya's mom was yelling because she did not want him to leave, and he was shouting because he didn't want to go but felt he had to. Her dad was pleading for them to go with him, but Sheila did not want to leave Florida. Richard was only leaving to care for his sickly mom in New York, but Sheila was not having it. They were going back and forth until the argument stopped and he walked out the door.

Next, she saw his image backing away in a smoke-filled room. The smoke was getting thicker, and his image was vaguely visible. He faded away into a white moving haze, symbolizing he was gone.

That vision of her dad leaving jolted Caniya out of her sleep. Waking dazed and emotionally drained, she looked around her room, and tears began to fill her eyes. She realized she had been dreaming, except the first part of the dream with her parents arguing had been a real memory. Holding back her tears and trying desperately not to cry was her main concern. Again, she began talking to herself and taking deep breaths to gain control of her emotions.

Speaking out loud, Caniya sadly said, "Why couldn't they find a way to make it work? They don't realize the effect on me by not having my father here. All I have to remember him by is this old photo."

Caniya pulled out the photo and moved her fingers over the image of her and her dad. She cherished the photo so much that she carried it with her every day. Wherever she went, it went…*period*. She kept his picture in her cell phone case. One thing for sure is she was never without her phone, so he was always with her.

After those thoughts of missing her dad subsided and she returned the photo to its special place, she could no longer hold in her tears. Water began to fill her eyes and spilled down her face. She cried for just a minute, wiped her face, sucked it up, took a deep breath, and said with a firm voice, "Caniya, get it together. You are on a mission. Finish packing your bag and get out of here!"

Caniya lingered a bit longer, sitting on the edge of the bed. Then with a sense of urgency, she jumped up and started packing for a second time. She looked at the overly stuffed mini suitcase and began struggling to get it zipped. A few more tugs on the zipper were accompanied by a few more harsh words about her mom. "She is going to regret mistreating me. I'll show her…I'm out of here!"

Caniya stopped to scribble a quick note: *"I'm out! I'm gone! I'm never coming back."* She planted it where her mother couldn't miss it.

She grabbed her suitcase, her cell phone, and her designer Telfar purse; she raised the first-floor bedroom window and decided to first push out the suitcase, which landed with a dull thud on the freshly cut grass. Then she quietly climbed out to freedom.

There was no time to waste, so she cut through the backyard to avoid the nosy neighbors. She moved quickly, looking over her shoulders every so often.

Was she really doing this? The weight of doubt creeped in but only for a few seconds. No, she was not going back.

As she walked, pulling her suitcase behind her, she simultaneously took a deep breath and pulled her phone from her back pocket. Caniya hit up her best friend, Karden, on his cell phone, but he didn't answer. She took another deep breath and checked the tracker on her phone, thinking to herself, *I'm glad I can track him because I need him...now! He's not going to believe that I finally got up my nerve to leave. I can't believe it myself, so I know he's going to say, "Yo, you serious?" And I can't wait to say, "Yes! Big things ahead!"*

Looking down at her phone again, she could see he was at the park, most likely at the basketball court with his neighborhood ballers.

Caniya had met Karden when she first moved to Ridgely Estates in Jacksonville, Florida. They were both born on the same day and shared a lot in common, such as the same sense of humor, the same corky laugh, and the same love of tacos with a side of melted cheese. Over the years, they had become close, like brother and sister. Caniya looked out for Karden, and Karden forever protected Caniya. There wasn't a day that went by that the two weren't either hanging out together or on the phone. So, who else would she call? Her one and only ride-or-die. Her twin spirit and best friend forever more.

Although Caniya and Karden were best friends, they lived in different neighborhoods. A park divided their two communities. Ridgely Estates, where Caniya lived, was a middle-class neighborhood with single-family homes. Crystal Cove, where Karden lived, was known for its crystal-clear and inviting beach waters; however, over time, it became an area where your safety was questionable. You entered at your own risk or didn't visit unless you were invited. There was always someone breaking the law and being carted away in cuffs.

Crystal Cove was a lower-income community consisting of projects and apartments, but nevertheless, most of the residents were honest working people. Unfortunately, it had a heavy gang population, and you had to understand the population and lifestyle to maneuver in the environment. Most of the teens went to Ridgely High, and both communities hung out at Crystal Park, but those who lived in one neighborhood didn't venture into the other. Caniya never went beyond the park unless Karden accompanied her. The park was a convenient meet-up spot for them because it was midway between where they both lived. It was the one place where they both could sit and share their honest feelings and be assured that no adult or sibling was listening.

Caniya proceeded to walk to the basketball court, but she was consumed by the thoughts in her head. She wondered how she got to this horrible place with her mom. Memories of her past stayed collected, sorted, and filed in her head, especially the negative ones. However, a glimmer of happy visions started creeping into her thoughts. She recalled how beautiful and talented her mom was.

Sheila had skills and big dreams. Starting her own clothing line was her biggest ambition, but it just never happened. When Caniya was little, she remembered her mom getting dressed every morning. She would shower, lotion down, put on her makeup, style her hair, put on a trendy outfit, and top it all off by spraying the latest designer fragrance in the air and then walking directly through it. Caniya could remember asking her why she would spray it in the air and not on her body, and her mom would say, "Baby, walking through the mist symbolizes that I'm ready and prepared to step into my day with confidence and fearlessness." Then she would twirl in a circle and pretend to be on a runway and strut. After her runway strut, she would stand in front of her gigantic floor mirror and make sure everything was perfect.

First, she would make sure her outfit was right and her shoes and handbag worked together with her outfit. Then she would look at her hair to make certain it was flawless, and next, she would check her makeup to ensure the blend was spot-on. Lastly, she would look into the mirror, pucker her lips, and then throw herself a kiss; to top it off, she would put her hands on her hips and say, "Here I come, world...watch out!" She was so much fun, and Caniya adored everything about her in those early days. Her dad was with them too, but then he left, and some of the magic left with him.

Then everything changed when Sheila married Caniya's stepdad and they moved to Ridgely Estates. She vividly recalled moving into their four-bedroom home on Plymouth Road in Jacksonville, Florida. Within an instant, a huge smile took over her face, and her thoughts shifted to her siblings, whom she adored. They both brought an enormous amount of joy to Caniya's world, especially when she and Sheila could not agree on something.

They bought her comfort when distress showed up, even though, as time went on, her mom favored them over her.

The disagreements started when her siblings were born. At that time, her mom's appearance went downhill, and her attitude about being fearless faded to black. Poof! It almost seemed as if her mom's dreams never existed. Caniya would have given anything to have her beautiful, brave, and playful mom back. As she continued to walk, Ridgely Vocational High School came into view. Ridgely, also known as VHS, was a vocational training center for a variety of trades, and Caniya attended their School of Fashion Design program.

Ridgley High meant so much to Caniya because she got to create original designs and then wear her own innovative fashion concepts. And she did wear them well! She was definitely a combination of Megan Thee Stallion, a hot rapper and influencer, and Tyra Banks, a model and fashion superstar. Caniya was built extremely well for her age, and she took good care of her body. She stood 5'7" with just the right amount of curves and hips for a sixteen-year-old. Her legs were slender and long like a high-fashion runway model. She wore long braids with colorful extensions that hung down to her waist and swayed from side to side as she walked. Every strand of her hair was always in place, and her edges were swirled to perfection.

Caniya's makeup complemented her outfits and her beautiful, light brown eyes. Her beauty and fashion sense were enhanced by her ability to talk about almost any teen topic, which she could back up with facts. These were her assets, and she knew it. These qualities gave her the strength to stand up for herself and influence others. This strength was needed to stand up to jealous girls at school, and she would also need it to endure her upcoming endeavors in fashion.

Although Caniya couldn't see it, she was the identical image of her mom when she was younger.

As Caniya passed the school, she pulled out her phone and checked Karden's location. She discovered he'd left the park and was now at his house. She was a little hesitant about going to Crystal Cove without being accompanied by Karden, but Karden wasn't answering his phone, and she needed him. Caniya took a deep breath, something she would do to help calm her anxiousness. Yet she picked up her pace to a jog and started humming to herself to avoid her feelings of fear.

Caniya concentrated on what she was going to tell Karden. She could feel the anxiety exiting her mind and joy replacing the panic as she anticipated the excitement of being around Karden's calming demeanor. Karden was the one person who could soothe the inner beast in her when she became unruffled. But what Caniya loved most about Karden was that he had street skills, something that did not come naturally to her, and that he was also intellectually gifted.

As Caniya approached Karden's house, she saw him sitting on his porch steps with his head in his lap. In her mind, she was saying, *I am super glad to see him, I'm safe!*

She called out his name, sort of like a song, "Kar-rr-dennn."

Karden didn't reply. Nevertheless, Caniya, still full of a series of emotions—frustration, fear, happiness, and anger—began to shout at him as she got closer. "Karden, let me tell you…" Before she could get the complete sentence out of her mouth, Karden jumped up and said, "Niya, stop yelling my name out here in these streets!" His face displayed panic and urgency.

Caniya could see something was clearly wrong, and Karden's tone of voice was not one she was used to hearing. The frantic look on his face made her shift gears instantly, and she realized that she needed to listen up. She really needed Karden's peace, but it seemed both of them were having a rough day—something she did not expect. Caniya could instantly feel her anxiety about to flare up, so she quickly sat down next to him with great concern.

Then Karden began to explain.

Chapter 2

DREAMS UNREALIZED – SHEILA

Kendall Jackson

Saturdays were for big breakfasts, cleaning the house, grocery shopping, and then a bit of fun, but this was not the usual routine for Sheila. The usual routine was fussing with Caniya bright and early on a Saturday morning. On this particular morning, she wasn't even sure how it began, but the words exchanged were front and center. They weren't pretty, as she always found herself lashing out at her daughter.

"You are not good enough to be a fashion designer and model. The competition is too much, and you're just going to get your feelings hurt. I wish you'd stop pressing the issue all the darn time."

"But Mom…"

"Don't *but mom* me! You need to do better around here with these chores instead of standing in the mirror all day fixing your hair and face. Ain't nobody gonna want you!"

15

Why did she say that? She would regret it later, but right now, she was on a roll. She saw the pain on her daughter's face but then… that face! My God, it was Richard's eyes, his nose, his height! Sheila was out of control, acting out of pure anger.

"You know what, Caniya? You act and look just like him, that man who abandoned us. Your father. *Ugh,* I hate it!"

Sheila stormed off, angry with life and angry with herself, wondering why her child, her oldest daughter, didn't act like her other kids and just do as she said to do. She concluded, "She's stubborn, just like her father!"

Sheila made her way to the kitchen and sat down, trying to calm herself. This model/fashion designer business is a dead end! She should know. It didn't work out for her, so how in the world would it work out for Caniya? Foolishness! The more she thought about it, the less calm she became, and then she found she had more to say.

She marched herself back to Caniya's room and barged through the closed door. She noted Caniya's eyes were red and puffy from crying, but she had little to no sympathy.

"Look, Caniya, I've always done everything for you since your dad left. I'm the one always providing for you, making sure you have everything you want and need. You're very unappreciative and disrespectful. I want you to think about how rude you are, and I expect an apology letter."

Sheila turned on her heels, slamming the door behind her before Caniya had the chance to say something.

Truth be told, Sheila had always been jealous of the bond Caniya had with her father, Richard, because Sheila never had the chance to build that bond with her own father. Sheila tried so hard to be the best mother. She didn't have too many pointers on how to do that because she grew up without a mother. Since her family was abandoned by her mother, her father became bitter and resentful, and he found very little to be happy about no matter how hard she tried to please him.

Caniya wasn't like her siblings; she sat in her room on her phone all day like any normal teenager, and if she wasn't on the phone, she was in front of that dang mirror! Bad enough that the walls were covered with magazine photos of hairstyles, movie and television stars, and wishful destinations. They were all just pipedreams! Sheila didn't like that. Caniya always felt as if she could never talk to her and was constantly saying, "You don't get me." Caniya was business-minded for her age, always coming up with plans to be a business owner, like owning her own cosmetics company and being independent. But she also spoke her mind, and that was something Sheila was never allowed to do as a child without getting in trouble.

Heated and mad about the conversation, she started thinking to herself, *Will she ever understand?* Before she knew it, she was bawling. When Sheila was a young girl, she had always wanted to be a part of the fashion business. When she told her father about her dreams, he would always shut her down, telling her that she would never work in the fashion industry. Caniya never understood how it was for Sheila because Sheila had never told her kids how it was for her growing up.

While she reflected on the Caniya chaos, the younger kids were out with their dad, Sheila's husband and Caniya's stepfather, Kirk Jackson. Sheila decided to lie down to attempt to calm herself, then she fell asleep.

After waking up from her two-hour nap, she finally thought it was time that Caniya knew about her past. It was clear that Caniya was determined to pursue her dreams, and while Sheila did not agree with them, they had to meet somewhere in the middle. Sheila knew she could never stay mad at Caniya for long, so she had no choice but to drop it. Regardless of their constant bickering, Caniya was an excellent student who loved her siblings, kept her room clean, and knew how to manage her money. Caniya wasn't afraid to work. She earned money braiding and styling her friends' hair.

Her husband and kids came home loudly, and the kids woke her up by jumping on the bed and complaining about being hungry. She went to the kitchen to start making the family some food. After the food was ready, she called everyone to come eat. After two minutes, all were at the table…except Caniya. Sheila stood at the bottom of the stairs and started calling for Caniya to come down, but she didn't get a response.

"Caniya! I know you hear me calling you, girl. Get down here."

No response.

Sheila's blood pressure started to rise again, and her voice went up a notch. "Don't make me come up there." Just when she was feeling better after napping, Caniya pulled this nonsense, ignoring her.

After several seconds, she shook her head and marched upstairs, ready for yet another confrontation. She was sure Caniya was still mad at her from the argument, so she entered Caniya's room and saw she was gone. Nothing was there but a little note on the mirror: *"I'm out, I'm gone, I'm never coming back."*

Sheila could not believe it. The note took her breath away, and she struggled to retain her composure. "No, no she did not do this!" With urgency, she checked the closet and drawers and looked for Caniya's favorite purse, which was nowhere to be found. There were definitely items missing, including her beloved makeup kits. A rare cool breeze caught her by surprise, and that's when she saw the window ajar.

Sheila started crying, believing she was the reason Caniya ran away. After reading the note again, she frantically called her husband to come upstairs. The tone in her voice forced him to come running.

Sheila was devastated. "She's gone. She ran away, and it's all my fault."

Kirk hugged her tightly, although he was shocked and confused about why she wanted to leave. In a nonchalant tone, he added, "Don't be so hard on yourself, Sheila. You know she's not going to be gone long. She will be back really soon."

Sheila felt like her husband didn't really care that Caniya was gone. Like it was one fewer child he had to worry about.

As tears fell down her face, Sheila started to realize he wasn't really being supportive, and that made her feel some type of way.

Kirk tried to sound convincing. "Look, I'm sure she'll be back in a few hours. Just give it some time. You'll see. She has nowhere to go. You know that girl is probably just trying to scare you, that's all."

She said to him with a tear-stained face, "You don't understand how it feels for one of your kids to run away. You don't understand how hard everything has been on me with Caniya, and you're still thinking about yourself because she's not your daughter. Whenever I go through something, you never ask if I'm okay. You dismiss it like my feelings don't count."

Sheila wasn't sure where all of that bubbled up from. Kirk stood there, stunned by her words. Sheila continued, "You better be right. I want my daughter back home, and if she's not here in two hours, I'm calling the police!"

She left Kirk standing there and went back to her bed distraught.

THE MAMA'S BOY – RICHARD

Kayla Mason

Richard was on the trail of what could be something or could be nothing. He had been following two men for the last twenty minutes. The two men had large duffel bags and wore hoodies, even though it was summertime. They just looked suspicious, and he had excellent instincts when people were up to no good. He called it his "spirit senses."

The suspicious men, both short and dark-skinned and wearing sneakers, would stop, chat for a few, and then continue walking. The problem was they had gotten off the bus at Port Authority thirty minutes ago and were still hanging around. Port Authority in New York City was not somewhere you just "hung around." Something was not right.

Richard hung back as much as he could. He tried to blend in with his six-foot stature, medium-brown skin, and short hair, which unfortunately was balding in the middle. He was a plain-clothes detective, so he looked just like every other New Yorker. Richard wanted to be a police officer because he saw the police arrest his brother, and it wasn't a fair trial. His brother was framed, and he was determined to be in law enforcement, where he felt there needed to be more honest policemen. He was going to be one of them.

The men went into the souvenir shop, and then Richard saw them create a scene and proceed to fill their duffel bags with merchandise. Richard sprang into action, called for backup, and handcuffed them, waiting for his fellow officers to take them away. He looked over and saw a little girl, scared out of her mind. She had the sweetest face, and his heart sank, for she reminded him of his daughter, Caniya, his "Baby Bear."

Richard had met Caniya's mother, Sheila, *way* back in high school. She was too cool for him and too cool to talk to, and she hung out with her clique who called themselves "Pretty Pink." All the girls in the clique wore pink—any shade of pink. Sheila was so beautiful. The first time Richard saw Sheila was at a football game for their school. She was wearing a short, hot pink skirt and a black shirt designed with hot pink letters saying, "Miss Me?" That outfit really brought out her beautiful chestnut skin and her shiny, smooth legs. She and her friends walked past him, going across to the bleachers. They had everyone staring, but Richard only had eyes for her. She had a boyfriend at the time, and he was the football captain.

Richard was at the game with his friends Mark and Troy, who had begged him to come to the game, and he didn't regret it because that's where he met Sheila.

Fast forward to their high school reunion five years later. Gosh…Sheila was still beautiful as ever. Richard was no longer that shy guy he was in high school, so he went up to her to have a conversation, and it was a good night. He took her to his favorite spot from high school after the reunion, and they talked until the sun came up, eating Florida's famous nacho hotdogs at Curious Carryout.

After that night, they were together all the time. If you saw him, you saw Sheila. One year later, she was pregnant with his beautiful baby girl, and three years later, he proposed to her. She was just so lovely, he had to put a ring on it. They were living a beautiful life with beautiful finances and a beautiful daughter.

Everything was great until Caniya was around the age of four. Sheila became verbally abusive towards Richard. He didn't really know where it was coming from. This wasn't the Sheila he knew. It would start with little petty arguments over taking out the trash or cutting the grass, and then it would just become a shouting match, no matter how hard he tried to remain calm.

Sheila would say things like, "You're less than a man," or "You aren't good enough for me," and other things that would make him feel down and not like the man of the house. One thing he knew was that Sheila didn't really like to talk about her feelings or her past; plus, she kept putting off an actual wedding date.

Richard had another flashback to that fateful day when he chose to leave his fiancée and beautiful daughter.

It was a phone call that no son wants to get. He picked up the phone, and it was evident something about this call seemed different, as all he could hear on the other end was crying.

"Hey, it's me, Kelly, your mom's neighbor. It's your mom, she's sick in the hospital. You need to come quick."

Richard felt hurt as he dropped the phone with his heart racing, and all he was thinking about was his love for his mother. He was scared that something bad would happen before he got there.

After the phone call, Richard went to the bedroom looking for Sheila to tell her the news. He was in tears, and he found Caniya sitting on the bed next to Sheila. Richard was a bit frantic, and his voice was shaky. "I just got a phone call saying my mother is sick. We have to pack and go immediately."

Sheila shot back, "Who is we? That's not my mother." Sheila said it like she couldn't care less.

Richard sniffled and grabbed some tissues and a suitcase. "I know y'all have y'all's ups and downs, but she needs me, and I'm not leaving without you two."

Sheila smirked and rolled her eyes. "You're such a mother's boy, always running to her needs. Choosing her over your family."

That caused Richard to blow a fuse. He yelled, "*She's family too!*"

Sheila shot up from the bed. "*She's not my family! You can leave.*"

Caniya started crying from all of the commotion. Richard and Sheila were staring each other down, and he took a chance. "I'm taking Caniya. No way is she staying here with you. You've been acting crazy around here. She's coming with me!"

Sheila's eyes grew wide. "You are the one acting crazy right now. No, you are not taking my daughter, and you better stop doing all this yelling in front of her. It's not making you look good, you sad mama's boy!"

Richard hated seeing his little girl cry. He did everything he could for his family, and somewhere along the way, everything started to go downhill. Sheila was just always in a bad mood. He didn't want to leave his family behind, especially Caniya.

Richard used a softer tone. "Sheila, you know I'm the only person who can help my mom during this time. My brother is in jail."

She had no response other than to scoop Caniya up in her arms and hug her tightly.

Sheila knew his family situation with his brother, and Richard could not figure out why she was acting this way. But then again, he did know why because Sheila had been acting really stuck in her ways, just being rude to everybody. Richard and his daughter were really close, like father-daughter best friends, and he didn't want to think it, but maybe Sheila was extremely jealous. Sheila would sometimes get that look in her eyes where you could see flames of envy.

After a few more seconds of no response from Sheila, Richard stopped communicating. It was going nowhere fast, so he continued packing his bag, even though he was hot and mad. He didn't want to leave without Caniya, but time was being wasted while anything could have been happening to his mother. Richard bought the next plane ticket to New York.

He went to kiss Caniya, but Sheila swung her around so that she was out of reach. He shook his head. "Sheila, I'll be in touch." To Caniya, he said, "I love you, Baby Bear." He waved goodbye to Caniya, who did the same.

"Goodbye, Richard."

During the whole two-hour flight to New York, Richard was shaking his legs and rubbing his chin. As soon as he reached New York City, he hailed the first taxi he saw. He was slapping the back of the seat, rushing the driver to drive faster to the hospital. Upon arrival, he ran out of the car, almost tripping over his bag going into the hospital.

"What room number is Alicia Brown in?" Richard asked the lady at the front desk.

"Room 213," the neighbor, Ms. Kelly, said, standing behind Richard.

Richard ran into his mom's room, dropping down to the floor, and holding her hand while she lay on her hospital bed asleep.

"Mom, I'm here. Please don't leave me." He said a silent prayer as the heart monitor started to flatline; five seconds later, a bunch of doctors came running into the room, pushing him out the way. Richard stood in the doorway, watching them resuscitate his mom while he held his hands close to his mouth, praying and begging the Lord that his mom would be okay.

After six hours, Alicia woke up. The nurse let Richard into her room, where he and his mom smiled at each other. The doctor came in and said, "So your mother will be fine, and she can be released in forty-eight hours, but she needs to stay on her medications, and she's going to need treatment. We will give you guys a call in three days to check on her. The nurse will come in here soon to have you fill out some papers."

Richard hugged his mom and kissed her while telling her how happy he was and how he had been begging God that she would be fine.

She weakly replied, "It's going to be okay, son."

Richard was so relieved, but his mood changed when he thought about how things were left with Sheila. He was thinking, *Perhaps by now she has calmed down a bit*. He decided to call her to let her know that his mom was going to be okay, but the call did not go as he planned or as smoothly as he would have wished.

"Hey, Sheila baby," Richard said with happiness in his voice.

"What do you want? Aren't you busy being a mama's boy?" she said in a sharp tone.

"I was calling to let you know my mom is okay, and I'm going to stay for a little bit."

"Why would I care, Richard? This has nothing to do with me. You left your family and home for your mother, and for what? For her to be okay in the end?"

And with that, Richard realized that Sheila really didn't care about what he had going on in his life, and she definitely did not care about his mother.

Richard was a mix of angry and sad. "I don't know what changed between us over the years, but your heart has become cold. I thought we could work it out, but I now see you have no love for me, and I am not going to stay with someone who has no compassion for me or for my mother." Richard choked back tears as he said, "Goodbye, Sheila. I won't be coming back. Tell Baby Bear I love her." He hung up the phone, leaving that life behind.

Loud sirens snapped Richard back into reality. The two criminals were being escorted out of the souvenir shop into a police van. Richard entered the shop and walked past the little girl and her mother talking with the policeman. He could see the little girl hugging her mother and crying to go home. As they left, he noticed a pink backpack on the ground covered in teddy bears. He grabbed it and caught up to the little girl and her mom.

"Hey, is this yours?" The girl nodded and took it as her mother said, "Thank you so much."

He watched them walk away, and his heart sank, for it reminded him of how he left Caniya. He took that as a sign that he needed to fix his relationship with his daughter before it was too late.

Chapter 4

THE B-BALLER – KARDEN

Preston Staten Hall

It was a typical Saturday morning. Seventeen-year-old Karden got dressed around 10 a.m. It was a nice day, so he put on his new blue Kyrie sneakers. He headed downstairs, where his grandma, Debbie, was making pancakes, sausage, and eggs for them.

"Good morning, Grandma. Something smells really good."

Grandma Debbie was so happy to see him. "Good morning, baby. I got your favorite meal."

After they ate breakfast, Karden said, "I'm heading out to the basketball court."

Grandma Debbie responded, "Karden, be very safe, baby. You know it's dangerous out there."

Karden nodded in agreement. "I know how important it is to be safe, and I know how much you want me to be safe."

"You know Grandma loves you."

"I love you too, Grandma Debs, and I might not say it, but I really do appreciate you taking care of me after mom passed away."

"Of course! You're my baby, just like she was at one point. You know, as you get older, you remind me more and more of her with your pretty hair and brown skin. But I won't hold you for too long. Have fun at the court, baby, and be back in this house before dark."

Karden's six-foot-one frame towered over his grandmother's petite presence. He leaned down and gave his grandma a kiss goodbye, and then he hit the streets.

When Karden left his house, he walked the same path every time. Karden thought a lot about what the future held for him, which he hoped included making it out of Crystal Cove. He was hoping his hoop skills would pave the way, but there was a lot of competition, and it was not going to be easy. Either way, he was determined to do it to make a better life for him and his grandma.

When he arrived at the basketball court, he sat his phone down on the bench, grabbed a ball, and started playing. He got out a few jump shots and layups. Then a boy who looked around his age walked up to him.

He asked, "Can I play ball with you? But I gotta warn you, I own this court."

Karden shrugged his shoulders. "Yeah, okay. What's your name?"

"Big G."

Karden noticed Big G was a little taller than him, and he was definitely heavier.

"Aight, Big G, here's the rules…no time-outs allowed. Each basket is a point other than the three-point shot. After a score, the other player gets the ball, and to get a three-point shot, you have to be behind that red line. The first player to thirteen wins, deal?"

Big G said, "Deal." Then he added, "You think you the best, but I know I'm better," as he motioned Karden to get the game started.

They started playing, and at first, it was basket for basket, shot for shot. Karden could tell bro was underestimating his talents. Big G was acting like Karden was a scrub. They were seriously balling. Big G was ahead by two points and started trash-talking. Karden let him talk. Then the momentum changed.

Karden got into the zone and could not miss. He was talking smack to Big G, telling him he was the best and to *put some respect on my name!* He was beating him. A crowd started to form, but that didn't scare Karden. It only added fuel to his fire.

The score was 11-7. Then Big G surprised him with a three-point shot. Karden wasn't about to lose this game, so he quickly scored and was one more point away from victory.

Big G took the next shot and someone in the crowd hollered, "Airball…get him off the court."

Big G didn't like that comment one bit, and he angrily tossed the ball to Karden.

The score was 12-10. Karden did a spin move and then dunked on him for his last point and won. He dunked that ball like Air Jordan.

Some in the crowd were cheering, but others were not impressed. Karden smiled, nodding his head like *I'm the man*.

Karden went to give him some dap, but it looked like Big G wanted to pound him instead. He looked mad, like an angry pit bull, but Karden wasn't no punk.

Karden put on a mean mug. "Yo, what's your problem, bro? I beat you straight up."

His opponent started talking like he wanted to do something. There was very little space between them, and then he did something Karden did not see coming. Big G put his hands on him and shoved him backwards.

Karden stumbled a bit and returned the shove with equal force, and Big G was pushed further back. The situation quickly escalated.

Karden said, "Yo, it's just a game! You wanna fight over this? Yo, I ain't scared of you. Your game is trash."

They started circling each other. Karden knew he was the lighter of the two, and soon he saw an opportunity. Karden punched him in the face, and the force of the punch rocked Big G backward then forward, then face-down into the corner of a bench. He hit the ground with a thud.

Karden looked around and saw people with their phones out, and as he scanned the crowd, his eyes settled on three rough-looking dudes. They started pointing and making hand gestures towards him. That meant things were about to get even uglier. Karden hadn't noticed earlier, but just then, he saw they were all wearing the same T-shirts and their arms bore the same snake tattoo.

Uh oh! Karden knew that one of the guys was the leader of the local gang in his neighborhood, the Viper Kings. He had no idea that Big G was part of that gang, or he would have never played ball with him.

The three of them were coming toward him light-ning-fast and talking about taking care of him, and he knew what that meant, so there was only one thing to do. He grabbed his phone off the bench and ran for his life. The whole time he was wondering if he was going to make it back home in one piece and how disappointed his grandmother would be if she knew he got into a fight.

Still, he ran as fast as his feet could carry him. He could hear a car screeching and voices shouting at him as he picked up the pace, never once looking back.

Chapter 5

THE CAREGIVER – GRANDMA DEBBIE

Camille Carmichael

As soon as Karden left, Grandma Debbie said a prayer that he would be safe and return the same way he had left. These streets were no place to be hanging around, especially after dark. Karden was a teenager, and she knew she couldn't lock him up in a room and keep him under her watchful eye. She just had faith that God would protect him and knew that boys needed to find their own paths.

Debbie was a retired nurse who loved the Lord. She really enjoyed worshipping and being part of the seniors' group at church. She attended seniors' group two or three times a week for Bible study and a crafts class, where she made soaps and candles with the other church seniors for extra money to support her retirement income. She had spent thirty-five years at North General Hospital but eventually she decided to retire, and she was thrown a grand party for her retirement.

Debbie sat down for a few minutes and watched her favorite pastor, T. D. Jakes, and then she did her devotionals. Afterward, she started cleaning up and looked at all her family pictures, especially Karden's.

Karden was her heart. She had been taking care of Karden since he was born. See, Karden's mom, Tanya, passed away right after giving birth. The doctors said that Tanya lost so much blood during the delivery that her heart stopped only minutes after holding Karden for the first time. Karden's dad, Camden, was falsely incarcerated two years after Karden's birth. Grandma Debbie lost one child and gained another. She was able to manage taking care of Karden while she was working, but when she had to retire three years prior, they unfortunately had to move to the lower-income part of town. Social security only went so far, and she had a modest retirement account.

Debbie dusted off a few of Karden's basketball trophies. That boy loved basketball, and she liked attending his games. He was always promising to make it to the NBA and move them into a better house and community. It didn't matter much to her as long as they were together.

She and Karden got along well. Saturday and Sunday morning breakfast was their bonding time. They often sat across from each other and talked and laughed about anything. She always asked Karden about his plans for the day, even though she already knew Karden loved to play basketball, especially on Saturdays.

Then she ran across a picture of her daughter, Tanya. It was her high school graduation portrait. Karden resembled her a lot. They both had big, beautiful brown eyes that sparkled in the sun, but the most identical feature they both had was a mole the shape of a heart on their cheeks.

Looking at that picture sure brought back some memories. She started thinking about the time she found out Tanya was pregnant with Karden. Tanya was a very free-spirited girl and was kind and incredibly fun to be around. She was popular and had lots of friends, but she could not stay away from the neighborhood boy, Camden. Camden and his brother always hung out in the same park as Tanya. They would be on the phone talking all night long and first thing in the morning. Camden was a nice young man but still not good enough for Tanya in Grandma Debbie's eyes.

After a while, Tanya and Camden started dating. Then it happened…Tanya came home one evening with him. Grandma Debbie was in the kitchen making chamomile tea when Tanya walked into the kitchen nervously and asked Grandma Debbie if they could speak with her. Grandma Debbie, already sensing it was not going to be good news, sat down in her favorite recliner and said,

"Spill it." Tanya grabbed Camden's hand and they shared they were having a baby.

Grandma Debbie was surprised but not shocked because she could see how much they cared for each other. They seemed so very happy, but she was worried as any mother would be. They were only in their early twenties when they had met—too young to have a baby. Five months later, Tanya and Karden found out their baby was going to be a boy. They were so excited and began looking for names. Camden suggested naming him George, but Tanya disagreed. It sounded too old of a name for her. Tanya suggested Elijah. Camden disagreed. He just felt that was not the right name for him. Camden suggested, "What about Karden, after the famous all-star football player who plays for the Florida Gators?" Tanya agreed. She liked that name for her son. Karden Emmanuel is what they decided.

Even though Grandma Debbie thought they were too young to have a baby, she was excited at the thought of being a grandmother.

The phone rang. Grandma Debbie was still reminiscing about Tanya, and when the phone rang for a second time, it snapped her back into reality. Grandma Debbie put Tanya's picture down and answered the phone.

"Debbie, it's Angela. What time will you be at church today?"

Grandma Debbie replied, "Oh, are we meeting today? I surely forgot. I'm not sure when I'll be there. Right now, I'm waiting on my grandson to come home."

Angela replied, "Okay, don't forget to bring the wicks. We can't make the candles without them."

Angela was one of those church folks who was in everybody's business, always bossing people around. Grandma Debbie replied with an attitude, "I know what to bring. See you when I see you."

Grandma Debbie hung up the phone and began to collect all her things and all the materials for candle making. Afterwards, she prepped some food to make while waiting for Karden to return. She thought about texting him but heard some voices on the porch. As soon as she opened the door, she saw Karden and Caniya sitting down, talking to each other.

She addressed them, "Karden, you're back!"

"Hi Ms. Debbie," Caniya responded sweetly.

"Hi baby. Oh, what a joy to see you today."

"You too," said Caniya.

Grandma Debbie loved Caniya. She felt she was good for Karden, as those two always had fun together. Karden was doing his best not to make eye contact. Their bond was so tight, he knew she could sense if something was wrong.

"Hey, Grandma. Yeah, finished up at the court earlier than expected. You heading out?"

Debbie said, "Wouldn't you know? It's candle making today. I have to get going to church. I'll just grab my things and be gone."

Karden, keeping his head lowered, responded, "Have fun at church, Grandma. I love you."

"I love you too, baby," she replied. Then she gathered her things and left the house.

Chapter 6

THE PLAN: TWO ARE BETTER THAN ONE

Dream Ford, Preston Staten Hall

As soon as Grandma Debbie came to the porch, Karden and Caniya knew to stop talking so that she wouldn't hear all of the trouble going on with Karden. She was barely in the car heading to church when Karden started talking about his morning.

"Niya! I can't believe you're here, but I am so glad to see you! Listen to this! I was at the court, and this dude named Big G walked up on me. He asked me if I could hoop and if I was any good." Karden leaped up off the steps, throwing his hands in the air as if shooting a basketball. Then he started pacing in front of the steps while looking up and down the block.

Caniya walked over to him and said, "Stand still, you are making me nervous. I came here to share my day with you, but it's clear you got something going on, too!"

Karden kicked an old soda can on the sidewalk about six feet down the street. He looked at Caniya and shouted, "It was an accident. It wasn't my fault.'

"Tell me exactly what happened and don't leave anything out." Caniya sat back down on the steps, awaiting his story while producing her own movie in her head. Caniya wasn't just a creator of fashions. When her anxiety set in, she could create a whole murder mystery, sci-fi, or drama in her head.

Karden, knowing exactly who she was, said, "Stay calm. I think we should go in my house to have this conversation. We are not safe outside. I hung out here to make sure I wasn't being followed and then because I was trying to figure out how to avoid Grandma Debbie."

Karden grabbed her hand and led her up the front steps and into the house. He guided her into the kitchen and motioned for her to take a seat.

"I want you to just listen, please. Just hear me out before you say anything."

Caniya agreed.

"As I said outside, Big G was up at the court. He asked me if I could shoot and if I was any good at balling. I responded, 'Facts,' and then told him, 'Let's take it to the court.'

"The game got intense, and we were battling up and down the court. Dudes started gathering around watching and making comments. Big G was getting mad because everything he was shooting would not drop. Dude even shot an airball, so you know that set him off.

"Soon it was about me finishing the game. I only needed one more basket to win. So, I started talking smack, and I knew I could back up every word of what I was saying. He tried to counter, but dude didn't have any game. I gave him something that he couldn't handle.

"Niya, you should have seen it. I ran up the court, I leaped straight up in the air, and with one big leap and with one hand…I dunked the ball right in his face. Big G had to take the L and take me laughing in his face.

"At that point, bro lost it. He was ready to fight. I tried to walk away. I told him it's just a game, it's not that serious. It's simple—you lost, and I won. Next thing I know, he pushed me.

"Caniya, you know living in the Cove you can't let a dude put his hands on you without reacting. Dudes in the community would look at me as weak and start being disrespectful, so I pushed him back. We started fighting, and

I saw an opportunity to throw a blow to his face, and what a blow. Big G went down. He hit his face on the edge of the park bench. He was all busted up, and his nose was bloody," Karden sorrowfully announced.

"Then everyone at the court started gathering around him. I heard someone in the crowd say something like, 'We need to take care of him.' Niya, they were pointing at me! Turns out Big G is a part of the Viper Kings gang. It only took me a few seconds to realize I needed to run for safety, and that I did." His voice expressed fear.

"There was a group yelling, 'You can run, but we will find you. We know you from the hood. We gonna' get you!'

"I took off running and didn't look back. I could hear cars revving up and tires screeching as they took off trying to catch me. I heard someone saying, 'Spin the bend, I think he went down this street.' He turned the corner almost on two wheels, but I cut down a few yards, hopped a few fences, and lost them…for now."

Karden paused and started right back up. "They have no idea where I live. Not yet anyway. But it won't be long before they find me. This hood is too small for them not to locate me. It's just a matter of time. What should I do?" Karden was now speechless and seeking a suggestion from Caniya.

Caniya thought quietly for just a moment. She looked at him dead in his eyes and said, "We need to leave. No!

We've got to leave. Not tomorrow or next week…right now! You got away today without getting hurt, but what happens tomorrow when someone sees you on the streets? It's like the gods are telling us both to go."

"Caniya, what do you mean, the gods are telling 'both' of us to go?" Karden looked at Caniya puzzled.

Caniya didn't hesitate. "Listen up. Pack your bags! Seriously, go pack your bags!"

They moved from the kitchen, and Karden went upstairs and started grabbing stuff. Caniya sat on the hallway steps and began to talk to him in the loudest voice possible.

"I am going to start looking for the cheapest transportation out of Jacksonville, and I'm thinking it's going to be a bus ride for sure," Caniya yelled confidently.

Karden yelled back, "Niya, can you please, right now, without stopping, tell me what is going on and why you need to leave too."

"By the way, don't forget to pack your lucky sneakers," Caniya instructed.

"*Niya*! Stop playing!" From the top of the stairs, he threw a pillow down the stairs at her.

"Okay! Okay!" She tossed the pillow back up the stairs. "I thought my reason for leaving Jacksonville was major until I listened to you. I came to tell you I was leaving today and to try to convince you to come with me, but there is no convincing needed." Caniya burst out laughing and then said, "You got to admit, this is kinda funny that both of us need to get out of here."

Karden snapped back, "It's not funny. Sometimes you have a sick sense of humor." He came downstairs and sat next to her. "Now stop avoiding telling me about your situation. What happened?"

Caniya sighed. "It's my mom, as usual. We just don't see things the same way. I feel like I am disappearing. My mother has gotten on my nerves so bad that I've decided I can't be successful being around her. She's so negative and has too many complaints about her life. I don't think she even likes herself anymore. I know she doesn't like me because of the mean things she said today, and I know I definitely remind her of her broken dreams and my dad. Everyone says I look a lot like him. Maybe that's why she thinks I can't do anything right. You think it's because my dad didn't do things her way and she thinks only her way is the right way?" she asked Karden without giving him time to answer before she continued her conversation.

"She's bitter about her life choices and takes it out on me. I've got to at least *try* to make my own dreams come true. Strange how things work out. We both need to leave to better our lives."

Karden walked back to the top of the stairs. "Your mom is cool. I'm not sure why she treats and makes you feel some kind of way. Maybe after you become a great designer, she will see dreams are possible at any age, but yo, I'm about ready."

Karden added, "Oh yeah! Speaking of bag, how much money do you have on your Cash App?"

Caniya responded, "I have $100 on the card and $650 sitting in my Cash App savings."

That question prompted Caniya to think about how much her mom had been a good financial influence on her. As much as she and her mom didn't get along, she always gave Caniya an allowance once she completed her chores and taught her the value of money and how to save. She had been receiving a $25 allowance each month since she was 14. Her mom might have been messy in other areas, but she was savvy with money. She taught Caniya to put half of her earnings into a savings account for an emergency and to help fund her wants. She told her that as her parent, she would always fund her needs, but that at fourteen, Caniya needed to fund her wants. She taught her to always think about the future and never, ever be broke. That's why she used her talents in other ways, so that during those months when her mother wasn't trying to give her any cash, she could rely on her other skills.

Caniya didn't always listen, but when it came to financial independence, her mom was fierce. She was a boss. She had money but never got to use it to live out her dreams.

Karden walked back to his bedroom to complete his packing and do a check to ensure he didn't forget anything. He packed shirts, pants, Kyrie Irving sneakers, a few caps, underwear, and toiletries. He had to bring his Jordans; there was no stopping him on the court without them. Plus, he was thinking he might have to play a few games for money while he was on the run to survive.

Next, he went to his closet to get a few hoodies, and he faintly heard Caniya speaking. He responded, "If you want me to hear you, turn up the volume."

"Shut up, boy! I know I have a soft voice, but you can hear me. Now answer my question from a minute ago. How much money do you have for us to be ghosts?"

"Right now, I have around $300. My biggest worry is I know they are going to hurt me if they find me and then what they might do to Grandma Debbie. Big G is a part of the Viper Kings, and they protect one another. If you hurt one of them, they are coming for you and your family."

Karden paused with fear in his voice and then said, "They are notorious for crime and violence. We need to go!"

Karden slammed his small suitcase shut. Then he looked around the room one last time to make sure he hadn't forgotten anything and went downstairs. They gathered back in the kitchen.

Caniya shared what information she had found. "There is a Greyhound bus leaving Jacksonville at 6 p.m. It's now 4 p.m., so we have time to get there. The bus is going to New York City, and it will take us fifteen hours to get there."

Karden looked perplexed. "Whoa, did you say New York City? Why New York?"

Caniya cocked her head sideways. "Seriously, Karden, I can't believe you asked why New York? Why *not* New York should be the question." She chuckled. "It's the fashion mecca, and that's where I need to be to succeed. Who knows? I might get discovered just walking down the street, and then we'll both be set."

Karden laughed while still feeling hopeless. "Well, that sounds okay, I guess. I don't have a better choice at the moment. Whatever you think is good. I'm still trying to work through all that just happened at the court. And my main concern more than Big G is my grandmother. She means everything to me, and I'm her everything. Do I just leave without saying anything? What will this do to her?" Karden had more questions than answers.

Caniya sweetly said, "Calm down. You are overthinking this. I know you worry about your grandmother, but it will be better for her to miss you than for her to have to visit you in the hospital or worse. Let's just hop on the bus that's leaving at 6 p.m., and once we are on the bus, we can plan what we are going to do in New York City. If it makes you feel better, leave her a note like I did for my mother. But don't give any details of where we are going. C'mon, it will be exciting."

Karden looked around his home. He never thought he would have to leave this way. But he didn't have a choice. He proceeded to leave his Grandma Debbie a note:

Dear Grandma Debbie. I got into some trouble on the court, and I'm with Caniya. I'm somewhere safe, and I'll call you when I can.

As he held the note, Karden felt like he didn't really have time to think things through. "Caniya, I'm not so sure about this New York trip. I don't know anybody there. I'm not sure."

Caniya's tone softened, noticing her best friend was not as ready to leave as she was. "Trust me, you don't want to be here when the Viper Kings show up. I have it figured out."

Karden shrugged his shoulders and caved in. "Okay, how are we getting to the bus station?"

"We can go to Ridgely. There, we can get two scooters and ride to the bus station. Scooters are always at the school, so there are no worries about transportation. The only worry we have is getting to Ridgely High without being spotted by the gang, my mother, my stepfather, and your grandmother."

Karden blinked a few times listening to everyone they had to avoid. He scratched his head. "Alright. Let's get out of here before I change my mind."

Caniya pulled her hair back in a ponytail and put on a solid black baseball cap. She was wearing ripped baggy jeans and a black belly shirt. Karden was wearing a solid black hoodie with black jeans and black Air Forces. They decided to disguise themselves with whatever they had on hand. Karden pulled his hoodie over his head and then they both put on black sunglasses.

He looked at Caniya and said, "Are you ready?"

Caniya responded, "Let's do it!"

Karden left the note on the kitchen table amidst several pieces of mail.

Chapter 7

THE ESCAPE

Dream Ford, Preston Staten Hall

While Caniya seemed happy to get away, Karden was in a different place. He never ran away from a fight, but in this case, there were a whole lot of them and only one of him.

Caniya and Karden peeked out his front door and looked both ways to make sure everything looked safe. As far as they could see, everything looked normal. Karden said, "I don't see any of them. Let's head to Patterson Park." They knew once they passed the park they would be in a safer environment. But they also knew that they had to get there first.

They were cautiously avoiding main streets and watching cars as they passed them by. Karden saw a car coming toward them and it looked like the same one from earlier. Karden started to panic but managed to calm himself down. He was feeling like they were in big trouble, but he didn't want to worry Caniya. The car got closer, so Karden pulled his hoodie tighter and stopped. He bent down to act as if he was tying his shoe.

Karden whispered to Caniya, "Come closer." He was on one knee looking dead straight at the ground but quietly started speaking to Caniya. "Is that a black Honda with tinted windows?"

"No, it's not a Honda, and it's blue," Caniya confirmed as she sneaked a peek at the car.

"That was close!" Karden's face glistened with sweat from his hoodie and the Florida heat.

"Too close!" Caniya agreed. "I'm getting a little scared."

Karden replied as bravely as possible being in such a situation, "Don't worry, Niya, I got you."

They proceeded on their way, moving strategically to the park, which was a five-block walk. Karden kept feeling as if someone was following them, and he wasn't wrong.

He whispered to Caniya, "I think the guy behind us in the red shirt is tailing us. I need you to stay calm and listen to my plan."

Karden started walking faster and Caniya struggled to keep up with him. "We are going to have to split up for your safety."

Caniya's upbeat personality was fading fast. "*No, we can't split up. I don't want to…please.*" The realization of this situation with Karden was starting to turn into them being on the news in a bad way. Caniya's heart was beating fast like she had run a race.

Karden said sternly, "You are going to have to trust me."

"Karden, I am really scared for you and what they might do if they catch you. If he follows me instead of you, I'm going to start running, and if he catches me, I'm going to give him some of this!" Caniya pulled out a tube that looked like lipstick, but it was pepper spray. However, she still didn't look up to the challenge as tears pooled in her eyes.

"*Niya! Breathe!* You have always trusted my instincts. I trusted you with this New York trip, so I need you to trust me right here, right now. Okay, we are on Ashland Avenue. When we get to Broadway Crossing, you go right, and I will keep straight to the next street, which is Casger Street, and make a right also. I need to see if he follows me, and if he does, you for sure will be safe. Once you turn down Broadway Crossing, keep going to the park. Don't stop and talk to anyone. If anyone speaks to you, don't get nervous. Just keep it moving. I'll meet you at the park. Now go!"

Caniya was terrified, but she knew Karden needed her to do this and remain as calm as she possibly could. So, she turned onto Broadway Crossing, and halfway down the block, she saw the red-shirted guy continue on Ashland. Her fears started subsiding, but her worry for Karden began to set in. She kept walking and praying he would be alright.

Meanwhile, Karden was still on Ashland Avenue, but he kept his head on swivel. He could see Casger Street in the near distance, but he could also see the threat keeping up with his pace. He made a quick right onto Casger Street, and so did the dude. Then Karden ran to the middle of the block and randomly sat on someone's steps. Karden was thinking to himself, *If this dude approaches me, what am I going to do? Should I get up and keep it moving or wait to see if he walks past me?* His instinct told him to sit on the steps and deal with the situation.

Karden was street-smart and hard, but not a gun-toting type of guy. His exceptional strengths were his charisma and being able to talk his way out of *most* situations, and that skill helped him maneuver in the streets.

Karden's thoughts were all over the place. *Man, you can do this. Just sit here, and whatever happens, happens. If he's coming for me, he's already let the gang know he's spotted me. There is really nothing I can do but wait to see if he walks past me.*

The Florida heat had him feeling like he was in a sauna, so he pulled off his hood to catch some air. The red shirt got closer and closer. He could now make out his facial features, which he did not recognize.

The dude was within inches of the steps where Karden was sitting, and soon, he was right in his space.

"Hey man, I was trying to catch up with you. I don't mean you any harm but aren't you the guy from the court earlier today?"

"Yes. Who are you? You been following me for about three blocks," Karden said calmly, although he was afraid.

"I'm Luke. I do odd jobs in the community. Look man, I know you know Big G's peoples are looking for you. Why are you out here walking in the open for someone to spot you? You see how easy it was for me to recognize you and follow you."

Karden answered, "I know, man. I'm trying to get out of here without being noticed by them. Any ideas?"

"First, where you headed?" Luke asked.

Karden thought to himself that he didn't know this guy and that he could be part of the gang.

Karden replied, "Not sure."

Luke said, "Wherever you're going, take Broadway Crossing towards the park. I started following you because I saw a group of them headed towards Bill's Corner

Store. Then I saw you walking. Y'all were one block away from each other. Just get off the streets as fast as you can. They are out looking for you."

"Thanks, man. I appreciate you," Karden said as he tapped Luke.

"You be safe, bro," Luke responded.

"Bet!" They both parted ways, and Karden took Broadway Crossing, heading to the park.

Now Karden's focus was on Caniya and her location. He instantly called her and gave her the details. Caniya was almost at the park, and Karden was ten minutes behind her.

Finally, Caniya arrived at the park and could see Ridgely High in the distance. The excitement of getting there without any problems prompted her to start running to get to the school. Karden was now within eyesight of the school. He looked as far ahead as he could to see if he could spot Caniya, but he didn't see her. He walked to where the scooters were located and…there she was!

Karden looked at Caniya and Caniya back at Karden, and together, they felt relieved.

Karden said, "We still must get from here to the Greyhound bus station. We should also turn off the tracker on our phones and silence all notifications."

Caniya hadn't even thought about all that and quickly disabled that functionality, as did Karden, but she had been so mad earlier that she had already blocked her mother.

They grabbed two scooters and paid for them. Once they were secure with their bags and ready to take off, Karden said, "Stay close, and watch out for these cars." She nervously nodded, and they took off.

Chapter 8

THE JOURNEY

Dream Ford, Preston Staten Hall

"Pull in right here!" Caniya yelled as they arrived at the bus station. "We can just leave the scooters on the street. The bus doesn't leave until 6 p.m. What time you got?"

Karden parked the scooter and said, "Let's go inside and get our tickets. It's 5 p.m."

After purchasing their tickets, they decided to take a seat and catch their breath. Karden turned to Caniya and questioned her next step in the plan.

"Niya, what do we do for an hour? I know we are pretty much safe here, but I won't be comfortable until we are on the bus and it's pulling out of the station."

"You hungry? I spotted a taco spot across the street when we pulled up. You got a taste for our fave? Nachos with a side of cheese! Bay-bee, I can already taste them," Caniya laughed out loud.

"Yup, let's go, and you can fill me in more on what's going on with your mom. What happened that prompted you to leave? I knew things were bad at times and you have spoken of leaving before, but I didn't think you were serious," Karden said with total concern.

Caniya's giggles quickly flipped to sadness as she explained, "You know how much my fashion career means to me, right? My mom just doesn't get it. She's controlling and doesn't listen to what I'm saying. She always thinks she knows what's best for me because she is the parent, but that isn't always true. I just can't get her to understand that I have a vision for my future, and even if she had the same vision and it didn't work out for her, it doesn't mean that my goal won't work out for me. I just wish she would hear me out without interruption. She is determined that I do things her way. I'm so over it."

Karden gave his opinion from a compassionate place. "I get you, Niya, but life from our perspective is hard for adults to understand. It's just that they get old and stuck in their time and their experiences. I think your mom really wants you to make it, but she is afraid of you being disappointed and hurt if you don't make it. I see both sides."

"Yeah, yeah, yeah, whatever, Karden. Wait. Are you siding with my mom? I know you are not taking her side. I get what you are saying, but my decision to leave is the result of us not being able to resolve our differences. The energy that was created after our big blow-up this morning is what's driving me to prove my point to her. So, here I am about to take the biggest chance so far in life. Let's not talk about it anymore. I want to get some nachos and relax, and the only way that is going to happen is for us to stop talking about this morning's argument with my mom." Caniya stopped talking, took a deep breath, and said, "Come on, let's eat."

They walked across the street, placed their order, and decided to eat in. Caniya pulled out her phone and checked the details of their bus ride. She noticed there was one transfer during the duration of the ride, and she shared the information with Karden.

"Wow, I just noticed once we get to Washington, DC, we will have to transfer to a Megabus. That also means we will have to buy another ticket. And that means more money. I hope you brought your lucky shoes because you are going to be on the courts in NYC making us some money. Just no more incidents, please!" She smiled devilishly.

Karden responded by poking Caniya in the arm and saying, "You not about to treat me like that. You better have a way to make some money, too!"

Caniya replied, "Whatever! Let's look at all the trip details before we go back to the bus station. I think we need to know what's ahead of us. Don't you?"

"Yes, I agree." Caniya shared her view of the phone with Karden. "We leave in thirty minutes, and then we'll be on the bus with no stops for fifteen hours. We will change buses in Washington, DC, and then we have another four hours before we get to New York."

"Let's go ahead and get our Megabus ticket now, what do you think?" Karden asked.

Caniya chimed in, "Hmm. I think we should wait until we get to DC. All seats on the Megabus are sold as a reservation with a specified time and date and that means no refunds. The Megabus runs every hour, and if for some reason the Greyhound is running late, we won't have to worry about losing our money if we buy the tickets once we get to DC."

At this point, Caniya and Karden made their way back to the bus station. They went straight to the departure terminal and looked for their bus. Their bus had started boarding.

Caniya was excited while Karden was still a little apprehensive about leaving Grandma Debbie. Caniya was walking extremely fast, but Karden had slowed down and fallen behind her. She turned around and saw him looking doubtful.

She reached for Karden with her hand out and he grabbed her hand. She pulled him close and said, "We are going to be fine, and our families are going to be alright. This is just temporary. We will return when the time is right. Now you must trust me."

Looking uncertain, Karden replied, "Yo, you know we close anytime I look like I'm going to cry around you. And you betta not tell anybody." He smiled and got himself together. "My heart is hurting, but I know this is the right thing to do. Circumstances are making me do things I don't want to do. I'm starting to sound just like Grandma Debbie. It's hard to leave her though. She's going to be so worried."

Caniya nodded and said, "I hear you, but it's now or never."

Karden agreed, and they boarded the bus. Once everyone was seated, the driver started the engine and pulled off.

"There is no turning back now," Caniya joked.

Karden simply replied, "You're right." He rested his head back on the seat and closed his eyes, realizing how much he had been through in the last ten hours and how much it had drained him.

Karden got quiet, and his body began to relax. Next, he felt his mind relaxing, too. He looked down at his phone to check the time and saw it was 7 p.m., and he never looked back up. Karden's quietness quickly changed into sleep.

Caniya, being the organizer and planner, continued to review her mental notes on their survival once they arrived in New York. That didn't last for long. Her head got heavy, and she leaned toward the side passenger window. She could feel her body telling her it was nap time, but she kept trying to resist.

Unable to fight her fatigue, she laid a folded shirt from her bag on the window, gently placed her head against it, and shut her eyes. Her body followed.

C h a p t e r   9

A REALITY CHECK – SHEILA

Camille Carmichael, Kendall Jackson

Hearing a knock at the door, Sheila sat straight up out of her bed even though she did not know who it was. Her husband said he would get the door so she could finish resting. It was a police officer wanting to talk to Sheila about Caniya. She ran to the door.

The officer was very official. "Hello, Mrs. Sheila Johnson. I have some bad news about your daughter Caniya. They found her body near the main road, close to the bus stop. I'm sorry, ma'am, but your daughter is dead."

The officer handed Sheila the purse they found that belonged to Caniya. Her heart dropped, and she fell to the floor screaming and crying. She proceeded to throw things across the room, squeezing the purse like it was the only thing she had left of Caniya. Her husband grabbed her and held her in his arms.

After hearing things breaking and a lot of screaming, the kids came downstairs scared, asking what was going on. After discovering the news, they all sat on the couch in tears and in shock, wanting to know how this had happened.

There was a loud thunderclap, and Sheila woke up from the terrifying nightmare. As usual in Florida, a rainstorm was moving through, only to be gone in an instant. Sheila found her phone and called Caniya again and again. She left messages and sent texts again, all pleading with her to come home, but unbeknown to her, Caniya had blocked her, and her messages went unseen and unheard.

"God, please let her be safe." Sheila tried to be strong so she wouldn't worry the rest of the family, hoping and wishing Caniya would come back.

After a few more agonizing hours, she had to do something. Kirk was not right about her daughter coming back. She went into Caniya's room to find any clues to where she could have gone, but she couldn't find anything. Looking all over the room, Sheila saw one of Caniya's favorite shirts on the chair. She picked it up and held it tight like Caniya was wearing it. Breaking down into tears, Sheila said, "God, it even smells like her still."

After that moment Sheila fell into a dark place, feeling like she didn't have the motivation or energy to do anything for anyone.

While Sheila was lying on Caniya's bed and holding the shirt, Kirk came upstairs and found Caniya's room door cracked open. He walked in, startling Sheila, who was sitting in the corner. He said, "Honey, get up and get it together. You're being weird, and it's starting to creep me out."

Folding the shirt and placing it on the bed, Sheila responded with, "You don't understand this feeling. You don't feel my pain or shame. I pushed my daughter away, and I can never forgive myself for that."

Kirk shook his head. "This is ridiculous." Then he left the room.

Sheila grabbed her phone and started making phone calls, repeating herself on each call: "Have you seen or heard from Caniya lately? She's been missing for hours, and I have no idea where she could've gone."

She started to look on Caniya's social media to see if she knew any of her friends in the photos Caniya had posted on Instagram.

She found a picture of Caniya and Karden on Instagram. She replied to one of Caniya's posts: "Hello, friends and family, have you seen Caniya? Please reach out to me immediately if you have any idea where she could be."

At this point, Sheila knew it was time to involve the police. She called the local police station.

"Precinct 174. This is Officer Smith. How can I help you?"

There was a brief pause, then Sheila began to speak with a shaky voice. "Hello, my sixteen-year-old daughter is missing."

Officer Smith instructed Sheila to gather some pictures of Caniya and come down to the station. Kirk tried to stop her, saying she was overreacting, but she wasn't having it, and there was no time to argue.

Sheila arrived at the police station and asked to speak Officer Smith. Standing by the copier, Officer Smith overheard Sheila ask for him and came up behind her. "Ms. Johnson?"

Sheila nodded, and he directed her to sit at his desk. Officer Smith asked Sheila many questions about Caniya, and even though she fussed with Caniya a lot, she knew every detail about Caniya from head to toe and knew everything she loved to do. The officer handed Sheila a missing person's report to fill out. As Sheila started to answer the first couple of questions, she started crying.

Officer Smith walked around from his desk to sit next to Sheila. He told Sheila that he would do everything he could to bring Caniya home. Even though missing persons reports were not to be filled out until after twenty-four hours of the person missing, this was a young girl out on these evil streets, and he was sympathetic to Sheila.

After two hours of speaking with Officer Smith at the police station, Sheila pulled her phone out of her pocketbook, and to her surprise, her phone was blowing up. It was people reposting the story about Caniya. That's when some of Caniya's friends started reaching out to Sheila saying they hadn't heard or seen her and were sending their prayers.

Sheila left the police station feeling sick. Her head was pounding from all the stress. It was getting late, and still no word from Caniya. *What was she missing?* Sheila suddenly remembered that boy, Karden. Yes, she had exchanged phone numbers with Karden's grandmother when they came over for the family Fourth of July cookout last year. With all that was going on, she hadn't thought to reach out to him. Finally, she called Karden's grandmother, Grandma Debbie.

Debbie was sitting in her favorite red recliner watching one of her favorite TV shows when the phone rang. She looked at her cell and the phone showed a number Grandma Debbie didn't recognize, but she answered anyway.

"Hello, who is calling?"

She heard a frantic voice say, "Hello, Ms. Debbie, this is Sheila, Caniya's mom. Is Caniya with Karden? She is missing…well, she said she was running away." Grandma Debbie could hear Sheila crying on the other end of the phone.

Debbie sat straight up. "Well, they were here earlier right out on the porch. When I got back from church, they were gone. I just assumed they went out to get something to eat. You say she ran away? My God."

Sheila was talking rapidly. "Ms. Debbie, are you sure they are together? Please call Karden and see when he last saw Caniya. Please call me back right away."

Debbie had a sinking feeling in her stomach. *No, that boy would not just run off and leave her.* She called Karden and got his voicemail. "Call me back right away, Karden." She wasn't a big texter, even though he had showed her many times, but she managed to type out, "Call me."

She waited five minutes. Ten minutes. Twenty minutes. No, this was not like Karden at all. Only when he was in school or playing ball did he not call back right away. She called again. No answer. She got up, knees shaking, and went into the kitchen to make a cup of tea to calm her nerves when something caught her eye on the kitchen table. She hadn't noticed it before, thinking it was a piece of mail, but it surely wasn't. It was a note from Karden. After she read it, Grandma Debbie had to hold on to the table to keep from fainting. She made her way back to her chair and called Sheila back.

Sheila answered on the first ring. "Yes, you found him?"

Debbie sadly said, "He's gone too. I found his note. Seems he got in some trouble today. Lord knows I wish I had seen it earlier. What are we going to do?"

They both were worried and scared not knowing where Karden and Caniya could be.

Grandma Debbie considered filing a police report too, but knowing that these two ran off together may not get her any sympathy or quick action from the police. She gathered herself and decided to call people who knew Karden to see if they had seen him.

Grandma Debbie tried to call Karden again and again, and still no answer. Only a few minutes had passed, but she thought she would call Sheila back to see if there was any news from her. There wasn't. Sheila replied, "No ma'am, but I will let you know as soon as we find her." Grandma Debbie hung up the phone with a heavy heart.

Grandma Debbie walked into her bedroom and sat on her bed. The last thing she remembered was Karden saying goodbye when she was headed to the church. She turned her head to look at the window and she noticed a picture framed with the words "I Love You" sitting on her nightstand. In the frame was a photo of her daughter, Tanya, holding Karden for the very first time and right before she passed away. Tears started to flow down Debbie's face.

Grandma Debbie decided to resort to a power greater than herself. She called Angela and the other ladies in her church group to pray for Karden and Caniya's safe return. Angela suggested they print some flyers at the church office to pass out.

Meanwhile, after the phone call with Ms. Debbie, Sheila had the same idea about posting flyers and went to create some on the computer. She didn't care what time it was. She was going to drive around looking for Caniya and hand out some flyers. Once they were printed, Kirk saw her grab her car keys and purse.

Kirk stopped Sheila, saying, "I'm glad you're up and about, but where are you going? It hasn't even been twenty-four hours. Caniya just wants attention."

Sheila became angry because her husband wasn't helping her look for Caniya. She told him, "You are not helping with any of this, so I gotta do what I gotta do. I'll talk to you when I get home."

Kirk responded with, "Will you, though?"

Sheila sighed, kissed the kids, and left on a mission to find her daughter no matter what.

Chapter 10

A NEW CITY

Dream Ford, Preston Staten Hall

Karden's constant moving around in his seat woke Caniya from her sleep. He greeted Caniya with a "Good morning." Then an announcement came over the bus speaker saying they were two hours from Washington, DC.

Caniya was surprised. "What! Two hours? I slept that long? I guess I was exhausted and didn't realize it. Wow! That was a good night's sleep. I feel rested. I still can't believe I slept straight through the night. Let me get myself together, and then let's talk about the transfer to the Megabus."

Karden replied, "No problem. Take your time. I'm enjoying the view on 95." Caniya went into the bathroom on the bus, and she did the best she could with the limited accommodations. She returned to her seat freshened up and with a quick wardrobe change, too. Even traveling by bus, she managed to keep every hair in place along with changing into another hot, trendy outfit.

When she got settled in her seat, Karden asked, "Did you know we passed Richmond, Virginia, a little while ago? And did you know Grandma Debbie has a girlfriend who lives there, and, in a moment, we will pass a huge amusement park called King's Dominion? I've been there before."

Caniya said, "I've been there, too. How do I look?" She did a mini pose in her seat.

"You look…alright, I guess." Karden knew his response would bother her, so he laughed a bit.

Caniya didn't think it was funny and replied, "Boy, stop playin' all the time, but I know I look good. I show up each and every day glammed and ready. I never know when I might be spotted. Now back to our Megabus conversation. Okay, since the Megabus runs every hour, we can decide when we want to leave DC and go to New York. I was thinking 6 p.m. That would give us time to have some breakfast and go sightseeing before we leave for New York. You hungry? I know I am. You in?"

"Yup, I'm hungry too, and I've never been to Washington, DC. This is becoming an adventure," Karden replied. Now that the plan for the Megabus was in place, they both sat back and enjoyed the ride, pointing out the great scenery.

They eventually pulled into the bus station around noon. There was a row of other buses. Their trip was extended due to several rest stops along the way. Everyone gathered their belongings to prepare to get off the bus. Karden couldn't help but think about Grandma Debbie and how worried she might be, but he still felt that him being gone was the best option to keep her safe.

"Wow, DC's got a lot going on," said Karden as they exited the bus. They had a couple of hours to kill while waiting for the Megabus to depart for New York. They decided to walk around a bit but didn't want to stray too far from the bus depot. They noticed a hot dog vendor on the corner. Caniya and Karden couldn't resist another opportunity to eat.

While they were sitting and waiting for the Megabus, they heard some music playing. Then they saw a group of teenagers with skateboards walking past them. They decided to burn some time and followed them across the street and eventually to a nearby park to see what they assumed was a skate park. They were right. There were a lot of kids in the skate park, and some of them were good with the tricks and jumps they were doing on their skateboards.

Karden really enjoyed sitting there watching them until they played the song *Dear Mama* by Tupac. As he listened to the song, he put his head down and started to get sad. It reminded him of how he had just left Grandma Debbie alone. When he looked up, he saw a woman, maybe a grandmother, giving three kids some food to eat. It made Karden remember how Grandma Debbie had taken care of him. He started thinking of all the things he would say to her when he was able to call her. He would let her know how much he loved her and would thank her for all the things he was grateful for. He cried one tear and said softly to himself, "I love you, Grandma Debbie." Karden hid his true feelings from Caniya.

Caniya excitedly told Karden, "This is really a cool skateboard park, and I would love to stay and watch some more, but I think we should get back to the bus terminal. I would hate to get this far and miss our bus to New York, New York!"

Karden replied, "I agree. We need to be heading back to the terminal, but I can't seem to get Grandma Debbie off my mind. I love her so much and hope she is not worrying too much. I feel so bad because I know she is stressing even though she is trusting in the Lord to watch over my every step. You know, Grandma Debbie always puts her trust in prayer and God when she is not able to control a situation."

"Yes, that's Grandma Debbie." Caniya smiled and said, "Let's try to keep our minds in a peaceful place by thinking all is well back in Florida and reminding ourselves that we will see our families again soon. Trust…everything is going to work out. I just know it is. I have this funny feeling in my gut that something great is going to happen. Every step we are taking is going to take us exactly where we need to be. So just relax and trust my instincts."

Karden gave Caniya a look of agreement followed by a smile. They grabbed their bags and started walking towards the bus station. The walk was fun as they tried to take in as many Washington, DC, sights and take as many pictures as possible.

They walked through the National Mall, where they saw a huge statue of Martin Luther King, Jr.

"*Wow!*" Karden was amazed. "This statue is gigantic! Take a quick pic of me. This is a moment that I want to remember," Karden said as he fumbled to get his phone out of his backpack.

"Hurry up, we still have to get to the terminal and buy our tickets," Caniya expressed in a hurried voice. She snapped the picture and they continued.

Next, they passed by the National Museum of African American History and Culture, where Karden took another picture, and they swiftly kept things moving due to their departure time.

Finally, they arrived back at the bus depot. They had ten minutes left before they needed to board the bus. "We need to get our tickets. They are only $20 per ticket. Get that CashApp card out. This one is on you. You got it, right?" Caniya said with a girlish grin on her face.

Karden joked, "Why are you always in my pocket? But yes, I got it."

Karden got in line while Caniya found them two seats to sit and wait for the boarding, but by the time Karden obtained their tickets, boarding was in motion. Karden yelled across the room, "C'mon, Niya, the bus is already boarding." As Caniya got closer, he exclaimed, "New York, here we come! I'm starting to get pumped up. We are exactly four hours and twenty minutes away from a fresh start for you and safety for me!"

Karden made a mental note that they were boarding the 6 p.m. bus, so it would be very late when they got to New York, but he didn't want to say anything just yet.

They boarded the bus, placed their suitcases in the overhead baggage compartments, and proceeded to take their seats. Karden stated firmly, "I get the window seat this time."

Caniya reluctantly agreed. "Okay, Karden, you can have the window since I had it from Florida to DC, and I doubt if I can sleep now that we are so close to our destination. I'm starting to get the jitters."

"Cool!"

They were excited to find out the bus had a new on-board entertainment system to keep them occupied. Karden was happy when he said, "We can watch movies and television, play games, surf the web, and listen to music all through our WiFi devices. Four hours is going to go by fast."

Caniya winked to acknowledge she heard him, and they both continued to explore the on-board entertainment systems. Caniya got comfortable adjusting her seat. She glanced at Karden, and he was jamming to some song on YouTube. She wanted to talk to him about her excitement, but he seemed to be enjoying himself so much that she didn't want to disturb his peace of mind. He had seriously struggled with leaving his grandmother behind. The music seemed to have put him in a joyful place. He was moving to the beat in his seat and had a big smile on face. So, Caniya thought it was best to keep her thoughts to herself.

The bus began to leave the terminal, and instantly, Caniya became antsy. Anxiety started to set in. She tried to find comfort by focusing on whatever was in her view as she looked over Karden out of the bus window. Her unease was taking over her mental state, and her thoughts were creating unsuccessful scenarios in head. She began to think, *What if I'm not successful in the fashion world? What if we run out of money? What if my mother doesn't care whether or not I return? What if we can't find our way in the dark streets of New York?*

Next, she started thinking about how in the end, she just wanted to make her mom proud and be a good example for her younger brother and sister, and she would love to at least be able to speak to her real dad one more time. She was wondering if it would be different with her dad and whether or not he would support her dreams if she were to tell him.

Then she heard a little voice in her head say, *"Just breathe. Just breathe."* Caniya began listening to the voice, and she could feel her anxiety simmering down. She continued to breathe deeply until she calmed herself down and her fears were lifting.

Caniya looked over at Karden, and he was still rockin'. She smiled and decided that maybe it would be a good time to shut her eyes and take a nap, and maybe by the time she woke up, she would be closer to her dreams. Caniya used her hoodie to keep her cozy and shut her eyes in the hopes that when she opened them, they would be arriving at Port Authority in New York City.

BUS TALES

Dream Ford, Kayla Mason, Preston Staten Hall

Richard was at his usual post in the Port Authority Bus Terminal. It was a quiet night. Many people were coming and going at first. Nothing out of the ordinary. Richard called for backup so he could take his break and get something to eat at one of the eateries. Sitting down with his salad with grilled chicken, he could see people getting off and on the buses and walking around the bus terminal aimlessly.

So many people were starstruck with New York City, but as a police officer, he knew the real deal. Many days, Richard sat there and laughed at some of the funny things he saw at the bus station, but this day was different.

While he was eating, Richard started to scroll through his social media and suddenly one of his memory photos popped up on his phone. It was a photo of him and young Caniya at the park. Richard felt heartbroken. He began to think again about how much he missed his daughter and how it had been years since he had seen her. He whispered under his breath, "Baby girl, I love you, and I am so sorry." First, it was the robbery in the souvenir shop with the little girl and now these memories on social media. Surely this was a sign and confirmation he needed to fix their relationship and to stop putting it off. He stared at the photo for five minutes and only looked up when someone came over and asked if they could use one of the chairs at his table. Because he was in plain clothes, they had no idea he was on duty.

Almost in tears, Richard regained his composure and put his phone down. Looking at the people walking past the eatery, he noticed two young people—teenagers or a little older. The girl was wearing jeans with rips in the legs and a black hoodie, and the boy was wearing all black. Working at Port Authority for many years, Richard had seen many come through dressed this way, and it was almost always someone trying to hide, especially during the summertime. He had barely finished his salad when he got up from his seat, took a last sip of his sweet tea, threw his remaining food into the trash can, and walked out of the eatery.

He had not taken his eyes off the two young travelers but kept his distance so he could monitor them. He was curious about them and wondered where they came from and where they were going. They stopped a few feet from the exit doors. They were standing there with a little bit of luggage, definitely not a lot for a prolonged stay. He saw the young girl pull out a phone and then start pointing to her friend which direction they should go. They exchanged words. The young dude seemed hesitant. They started walking to the left, and then they turned around and went to the right towards the train station.

Richard shook his head. He had seen this dozens of times—young people thinking they were ready for the big city, clearly lost. They looked so small compared to all the other people walking around Port Authority.

Richard could not take his eyes off these two. He radioed his partner. "Leaving the post for a few. I see something suspicious."

His peer replied, "10-4."

He stayed behind them as they approached the train station.

* * *

Karden and Caniya had just finished a back-and-forth discussion about where to go next. Neither one of them had been on a New York subway before, and with all of the signs, people, and pathways, it looked scary and complicated. As usual, Caniya tried to convince Karden to do things her way, and that meant heading to Brooklyn.

"Caniya, Brooklyn? Who do you know in Brooklyn? I heard it's not safe."

Caniya smirked. "It's about as safe as Crystal Cove. We are going to be fine."

"You keep saying that, but I don't know why we can't just hang here in the city. I read a lot about it on our way here. There is tons to do, and a lot is open late at night. You never mentioned Brooklyn before."

Caniya had a different mindset. She remembered that a few of the fashion models she followed on Instagram lived in Brooklyn, and she had her heart set on that destination for other reasons too. "Look, I got us this far," she said, a bit agitated. "We can come back to the city any time, but for now, we are heading to Brooklyn. You comin' or what?"

Karden was not convinced. "Do you know of a hotel or something in Brooklyn? I mean, this is news to me. Where are we going to stay? This is crazy." Caniya closed her eyes and exhaled. It was time to come clean. "Okay, you got me. Listen, there's a nighttime photo shoot in Prospect Park tonight, and I just want to be on the scene, you know, at least see what it feels like to be among some models who are living their best life. Then after that, we can come back to the city and find some place to stay. I have a few lined up, but I failed to actually reserve a spot. We can do that together on the ride back. Please say you're not mad with me."

Karden sighed, feeling swallowed up by the massive crowd of people. As soon as they made it to their Brooklyn destination, he was calling Grandma Debbie. Shaking his head and feeling like he had no other options, he said, "Whatever, Caniya. Lead the way!"

Caniya quickly hugged him and whispered, "You're the best," then grabbed his hand as they followed the signs to the Q train.

Richard was gaining steps on them and soon found himself walking side by side with Caniya. Keeping his head lowered, he put on a Yankees baseball cap to conceal his face. He then glanced over at Caniya for a brief second, then he looked forward again, walking at the same pace as the rest of the crowd. He then slowed his pace so that he was now walking behind them, his thoughts racing a mile a minute.

Caniya had felt a man's presence close to her, and they made ever-so-slight eye contact, but she didn't like it. She noticed he had on a cap and a green jacket. She quickly turned and saw he was still following them.

Richard continued to follow them up the ramp. Caniya turned again, saw Richard behind them, then she grabbed Karden's hand and squeezed it.

Karden looked over at Caniya and said, "Hey, why are you squeezing my hand like that?"

Caniya leaned in closer to Karden. "I think that guy in the green jacket is following us. He has been behind us since we started walking this way."

Karden quickly turned his head to get a glimpse of this guy in the green jacket whom Caniya was afraid of. Karden replied, "Yeah, I see him. Let's keep walking and when we get to the top of this ramp, let's go right and if he follows us. Then we are going make a run for it."

As they got to the top of the ramp, they went right. A few steps later, Karden turned his head again and saw Richard right behind them, pace by pace. He turned back around and whispered to Caniya, "Okay, Niya, we've got to get out of here because he's still behind us. There has to be more places to hide on the street."

He grabbed Caniya's hand, and they fled toward the exit.

Richard continued to follow them, and when they started running, he did the same thing. The two young people exited Port Authority. It was close to midnight in Manhattan. Richard could see them picking up the pace and knew they figured out he was following them. He did not want to frighten them, but he needed to make sure they were safe amongst other things.

As they approached the corner of 44th Street, they both struggled with having a sense of direction with all the tall buildings, traffic, and honking horns. Even late at night,

New York City was indeed the city that never sleeps. Karden saw a possible escape path.

Still holding Caniya's hand, he said, "We got the light, let's jet across this street and lose this dude." They both ran, and one of the wheels snapped off Caniya's suitcase, but they kept going. Richard was right there with them.

Caniya asked, "What now?"

Karden yelled, "This way…let's try and lose this guy." But "this way" was down a dead-end side street, and there was no way for them to know that was Richard closed in on them.

Chapter 12

NO WAY OUT

Dream Ford, Kayla Mason, Preston Staten Hall

Karden and Caniya soon realized they had no exit. Caniya was in tears. "This can't be happening."

Karden was not about to just give in. He asked, "Where is that pepper spray you had?"

Caniya nodded, and with shaking hands, she fumbled through her purse. For the first time, wished she was home.

Richard followed them, and once he saw them turn into the alleyway, he knew it was all over for them. Richard was now walking slowly. He knew the city, and he knew there was no exit. He headed down the alley.

Caniya and Karden stayed close to each other, and Caniya started to cry and screech, "*Help!* He's going to kill us."

Karden could see him coming, and Caniya held tightly to the pepper spray. Karden picked up Caniya's tattered suitcase and lifted it over his head a few times as if lifting weights.

"What…are…you…doing?" Caniya was stammering at this point from fear, yet Karden was cool. After all, he had beaten up a member of the Viper Kings. He wasn't no punk.

"Listen, Niya. When he gets close enough, I'm going to bash him with your suitcase and then you are going to empty that pepper spray into his face, you got me?"

Niya folded her lips in, sniffling and trying not to bawl. She responded weakly, "Okay, Karden."

Karden put the bag down for a few seconds and held her by her shoulders. "I trusted you, now it's time for you to trust me! And if you see a chance to run for it, do it and don't look back."

Caniya was hyperventilating. "I can't leave you. We have to stay to…"

Karden's emotions were in defensive Black Panther mode, and he didn't let her finish. "I promise, I'll catch up to you. Now let's back up as far as we can into the corner where it's dark. We are going to catch him by surprise." Karden was determined to give them a fighting chance.

They crouched in the corner of the alleyway amongst the trash, bad smells, and dumpsters and waited for the predator.

Richard was halfway down the dimly lit alleyway. New York was known for long avenues, alleys, and streets; some of them were more than half a mile deep. This one was no different. He turned on his flashlight as he got closer to them. He called out and prayed that he was right about his suspicions.

"Caniya Brown, is that you?"

Caniya and Karden were crouched down and looked back and forth at each other, confused, but then the man got closer and his voice got louder. "Baby Bear? Are you my Baby Bear from Florida?"

Caniya and Karden stood up as Richard shone his flashlight in their faces. Caniya's heart was beating so fast because when she heard Baby Bear, it sounded familiar to her, but she could not remember where she used to hear that from.

She asked him, "Who are you? How do you know my name?"

Richard exhaled and had a slight smile on his face. "You are my Baby Bear. I'm Police Officer Richard Brown, your father! I'm your dad."

Caniya had not seen her father in more than twelve years, so she was not sure if this man was really her father, but she thought, *How else would he know my name?*

Richard could see that the kids were very scared, so he pulled out his badge, but Karden wasn't buying it. He stepped in front of Caniya as a barrier. "How do we know you are who you say you are? I could buy one of those off the street."

Richard calmly said, "Okay, young man, you have a point. What's your name?"

"None of your business."

Karden was mean-mugging Richard because he just was not sure he was telling the truth.

Richard nodded. "Okay, okay, listen to me, Caniya. I really am your father. Me and your mother, Sheila, broke up when you were about four years old. I had to leave Florida because my mother got sick. Do you remember any of that?"

Caniya started to remember crying and seeing her dad leave with a suitcase. Her dream was also fresh in her mind. Karden had heard this story before, so he said with amazement, "Niya, this may be your dad. Take out that photo you keep with you."

Niya produced the photo in a matter of seconds. It sure did look just like him.

Richard insisted, "Young man, I am her dad and I'm going to ask again, who are you?"

Karden was slow to respond but then complied.

"I'm Karden, and we're best friends."

Richard said, "I see. Can I come a little closer?" Richard could have done so at any time, but he took it slow, and even though they looked like kids, he didn't know if they may have had any hidden weapons.

Karden said, "Okay." Richard could see Karden was trying to be in protective mode. He admired that.

Richard got an arm's length from them, and he stared at Karden, realizing how much he looked like his brother. He thought, *It can't be.* Just then, his partner radioed him.

"Brown, where are you? You still on that mission?"

"Yeah, please cover for me. I need some more time."

"All right. You owe me. 10-4."

Karden and Caniya looked at each other, starting to believe he was indeed a police officer, and he had the same last name as Caniya.

"Young man, where do you live?"

Karden replied, "I live in Crystal Cove in Florida with my grandmother." Karden was puzzled as to why he wanted to know where he lived so he asked, "Why do you ask?"

Richard never answered the question but came back with another question. "Who is your father?"

Karden replied, "Look, he's locked up. I don't even know him. He left when I was two or three years old. What's with all these questions?"

Richard couldn't believe it. "I think you're my brother's son. My brother's name is Camden. Was your mother's name Tanya?"

Karden's eyes got wide as he and Caniya walked toward Richard. Karden said, "Yes, that was my mother's name, Tanya Davidson. And I'm Karden Davidson."

Then he quickly put the pieces together. "Wait, are you saying you are Caniya's dad and you are also my uncle?"

Richard, overwhelmed by what was happening, stood there with his hand over his eyes and said "Yes," pointing his fingers at Caniya, "I'm your father…" and then to Karden, "…and your uncle…and you both are cousins."

The two smiled, looked at each other, and then hugged. Caniya said, "You're my family." Karden replied, "You're mine, too."

Richard said, "Whew, so glad you all aren't dating." The two separated quickly, making faces at the thought, which caused Richard to laugh and then add, "Now that we've gotten that out of the way, what the heck are you two doing in New York…alone?"

Chapter 13

THE REVELATION

Dream Ford, Kayla Mason, Kendall Jackson, Preston Staten Hall

When he asked them why they were in New York alone, they were silent. So, he motioned Caniya and Karden out of the alley and onto the street. All of them were still surprised by the recent events.

Richard asked them if they wanted to go to a nearby all-night diner to get something to eat. They both said "yes" simultaneously. Richard said, "Okay, let's go. And I want the full story about you two leaving Florida."

When they were seated at the diner, at first, no one was talking because they were hungry and exhausted. Richard couldn't stop looking at how beautiful Caniya was—a combination of him and Sheila—but she did resemble him a bit more. And then Karden had a lot of his brother's characteristics.

He let them order whatever they wanted, and they were happy to see tacos and nachos on the menu, so they both got their favorite. Richard settled for a tuna sandwich and a side of fries. He then got down to business.

"Okay, you two, what's going on?"

Caniya told him how she felt like her mother was always yelling and screaming at her. She told Richard that she wanted to be a model and that Sheila was always telling her that she was not pretty enough and wouldn't make it as a model. She explained that those words were hurtful, and she was sick and tired of hearing them and getting put down.

She ended with, "So I ran away. I wanted to show her that I could make it."

"I see." Richard looked at Karden and asked, "What's your story?"

Karden told him the story about the fight at the basketball court and how he feared for his life. He mentioned the Viper Kings, Big G, and how he wanted to keep his grandma safe. He talked about how Caniya showed up at his house already planning to leave, so it was easy to just leave with her.

Richard, understanding both of their situations said, "Listen, I get it, but you can't just up and leave without letting anyone know where you are. Do you know how reckless that is? I'm glad I was the one who noticed you, but what if it wasn't me following you but someone dangerous? You had nothing to protect yourselves. You just can't do things like that."

Caniya and Karden sat there quietly with their heads down.

"Have either one of you been to New York before?"

Caniya and Karden both shook their heads no. Richard asked, "Would you like to see a little more of New York before you go home?" They excitedly agreed. Richard thought that would be the case. "Well, before we do anything, I need to call your parents and let them know you are safe and will be staying with me for a couple of days."

After the diner, they headed to Richard's home, a two-bedroom apartment in Flatbush, Brooklyn. Caniya finally got to see Brooklyn. Richard decided to have a two-bedroom apartment so his mother had her own room when she visited from Mount Vernon. Richard showed Caniya where the spare bedroom was, and then he went into his hall closet and pulled out some sheets and handed them to Karden. "You'll be on the sofa bed for the next couple nights," and he pointed to the leather sofa.

When Caniya pushed the bedroom door all the way open, she could see photos on the two nightstands. She dropped her broken suitcase and walked over to the nightstand closest to her. She picked up a photo and immediately started to cry. It was a photo of Richard and Caniya in a park. She remembered because she had this same photo.

She saw another photo on the nightstand—this one of her mother and father. She could see at one time they looked happy. She was young when they split and never got the whole story about why they broke up. Still holding the photo of her and Richard, she jumped when Richard said, "You okay?"

Caniya turned the photo around so Richard could see what photo she was looking at. He chuckled and said, "That is my favorite photo. I think I have it in every room in this apartment." He came closer to Caniya and said, "You are so beautiful just like you mother." Richard promised that he would not let the distance or any disagreements with Sheila get between them any longer. Caniya, crying, walked over to her dad and gave him a big hug. Richard hugged Caniya back with tears falling from his eyes. "I'll let you get ready for bed."

Richard closed the door and found Karden fast asleep, not even getting a chance to pull out the sofa bed. He covered him with a blanket. Soon after, he checked on Caniya, who also was out like a light. After all, it was six in the morning!

* * *

Richard had a lot to do. He requested immediate time off for a family emergency. He had an excellent track record with his department, and he had never asked for time off before in this manner, so it was granted. But the immediate task at hand was calling Florida. Richard sat in his bedroom and called Sheila. She answered on the first ring.

"Hello?" Sheila answered the unknown number, hoping it was Caniya.

"Sheila. It's Richard." There was silence for a bit. She was a little confused, not knowing what to say to him after all those years. She had just returned from driving around again to see if she could spot Caniya and Karden.

"Hey, Richard. How are you? This is a surprise." She never even thought to try and reach out to Richard to tell him that Caniya was missing, and she was not sure how she would break the news to him.

"Sheila, I wanted to let you know Karden and Caniya are here with me in New York. I was working my post at Port Authority and saw them as they came off the bus."

Sheila started to cry tears of joy because she was relieved Caniya and Karden were safe.

He continued, "If it's okay, I'm going to let them stay with me for a couple days so I can show them around New

York. I have booked the three of us a flight to Florida on Sunday."

With gratitude in her heart and shame for the way she treated Richard when they were last together, Sheila said, "Thank you, Richard. Thank God. I know it has been a long time. I'm so sorry for the way I treated you the last time we spoke. I am so glad you found them."

Richard accepted Sheila's apology. "Yes, it has been too long, and I really should be in my daughter's life."

"You're right. Let's make that happen once they are home. Can I talk to Caniya?"

"Well, they are both asleep right now, but I will make sure they call home when they wake up. Can you let Karden's grandmother know?"

"Yes, of course. Thank you, thank you." And they hung up.

Chapter 14

SAFE AND SOUND

Camille Carmichael, Dream Ford, Kayla Mason, Kendall Jackson, Preston Staten Hall

Sheila started jumping and screaming full of joy and excitement. She was just so happy she couldn't stop smiling. She ran downstairs to kitchen where the kids and Kirk were preparing breakfast, and she yelled out, "They're okay and will be home in three days!"

Kirk was very confused, not knowing what she was talking about. "Who will be home in three days?" She was so excited, she forgot to tell them she was talking about Caniya and Karden.

"Oh my God, really?" Isis screamed out. Cole and Isis started dancing. Sheila ran to them, and they grabbed hands and started dancing in a circle. As Sheila looked at Isis and Cole, she was happy knowing all her children would be together again in just a couple days and they could be one big happy family. Kirk came over to them. "See, it all worked out."

Sheila cut her eyes at him. "You didn't even ask where they are! Well, Caniya is with her father in New York. So is Karden. You and I need to talk later."

Sheila asked Kirk to watch the kids while she ran to Ms. Debbie's house because she wanted to tell her about the good news in person.

Sheila drove smiling from ear to ear. "Thank you, God." She soon pulled up to Debbie's house and jumped out of the car so fast, she forgot to lock the car door and grab her purse.

She rang the bell, yelling through the door and knocking at the same time, "Hey, Ms. Debbie, it's Sheila."

Grandma Debbie opened the door looking sad and tired. "Oh Sheila." The women tearfully embraced.

"Can I come in?" Debbie nodded and they both sat on the couch.

Sheila could hardly contain herself. "Debbie, I have good news."

Debbie was hopeful. "Tell me you found them!"

"Yes, and they are safe. My ex, Richard, found Caniya and Karden in New York City, and he's bringing them home in three days."

"New York City," Grandma Debbie whispered. "How in the world did they get to New York?" she asked.

Sheila was shaking her head "Ms. Debbie, I have no clue, but Richard said they would explain everything when they get home on Sunday."

Debbie hugged Sheila, and they cried happy tears that their kids were coming back home.

Debbie pulled away and said, "Wait, we need to have a party."

"I'm glad to see we're on the same page," Sheila said.

* * *

While the kids slept, Richard ran to the store to get some food. He was a loner, so he needed to stock up his fridge a bit. He had never gone to sleep, used to doing all-night shifts, and seeing his daughter and nephew had him pumped up.

Late the next morning, the two runaways woke up to the smell of bacon and eggs. Richard usually went for a morning run, but he decided not to go.

"Morning, Daddy." Richard turned around with a huge smile on his face and said, "Good morning, Baby Bear." Karden sat up on the sofa and looked at them with a weird look on his face like he was looking at a soap opera. Richard says to Karden, "Come on, man, let's eat."

As they sat at the table eating breakfast, Richard told them all about the places he planned to take them while they were with him in New York. "First, we'll visit the Statue of Liberty, then we'll go to Coney Island, the Seaport, Madison Square Garden, Central Park, and then we'll hit Times Square." Caniya and Karden had no idea they could see all these places, but they were excited. He also planned for them to talk on the phone with his mother. He knew she would be so surprised.

After breakfast, he told them to allow their phones to get messages and fix their notifications. When they did that, they were shocked at how many people were looking for them. Text messages and social media hits were chiming all over the place.

Next, they each had to call home. It was easy for Karden to call Grandma Debbie, who cried half the time but was grateful for Karden's safety. But for Caniya, it took her a few minutes to call her mother. She went into the bathroom and shut the door. She closed her eyes to calm her nerves, then dialed her mother, who answered right away.

"Mom, it's me, Caniya."

Sheila was so happy to hear from her daughter. "Caniya, baby. I'm so sorry for how things ended between us. Let's talk when you come home. I have a lot to share. I was scared to death and had such a bad dream about something happening to you. I'm so glad you are okay. If I haven't said it lately, I love you."

Those words brought tears to Caniya's eyes. "Mom, I love you too."

They hung up and Caniya felt relieved.

Each day in New York was an adventure for Caniya and Karden. Richard kept them busy from sunup to sundown. The best thing of all was that they were one another's family—for real.

Chapter 15

FAMILY AFFAIRS

Camille Carmichael

No sooner than five minutes after Sheila had left Grandma Debbie's house, there was someone at the door. Grandma Debbie, thinking it was Sheila again, opened the door saying, "Did you forget something?" But as she looked up, she saw a man standing there. She squinted, looking up at the man, not afraid because he looked familiar, although she couldn't seem to remember who he was.

Grandma Debbie said, "Can I help you?"

"Ms. Debbie, it's me, Camden. Karden's father."

* * *

Camden had been at Cedar Correctional Facility for fifteen years for a crime he did not commit, but his bid was ending. He was just three days away from freedom, and all he could think about was seeing his son, Camden. While sitting in the community room looking at the TV,

Camden overhead two of the inmates sitting at the B-9 table mention that there was a scuffle at the basketball court in Crystal Cove. Camden knew his son lived in Crystal Cove with his grandmother, so he started to listen more closely. He heard them say that Big G got into a fight with some kid named Karden, and they were looking to put him straight.

Camden immediately asked the guard if he could make a phone call. He ran to the phone and called one of his homeboys, Frankie, who also lived in Crystal Cove. Camden was sure Frankie would know if anything had gone down at the basketball court.

When Frankie picked up the phone, he heard, "You have a collect call from Cedar Correction Facility," and he immediately knew it was his boy, Camden, and accepted the call. Camden didn't waste any time with hellos; he jumped right to it and asked, "Hey, you heard anything about some fight on the courts with Big G?"

Frankie chuckled a bit and said, "Well, hello and yes, I'm good, bro, but yeah, I heard about that."

Frankie told Camden that his brother, Luke, was at the basketball court when it went down and had the fight recorded on his phone. Frankie started to tell him the whole story about what happened with Karden and Big G. He told Camden that his brother, Luke, saw Karden running that same day as if he was trying to get out of Crystal

Cove. Frankie said, "Bro, you need to chat with Tiny to see if he can call Big G's crew off of Karden." Tiny was also incarcerated at Cedar Correctional Facility. He started the Viper Kings but also ran the B-9 crew at prison…and he just so happened to be Big G's older brother.

Camden said, "Thanks, bro," and he hung up and headed back to his cell. He lay back on the hard flatbed, thinking of his best approach with Tiny.

Camden had many encounters with Tiny during his fifteen-year bid in Cedar. There had been one incident where Camden saved Tiny's life after another inmate tried to shank him. Tiny had told Camden that he owed him one for saving his life and if he needed anything, to let him know. Camden, looking up at the prison ceiling, was thinking he may have to call in that favor.

The next day during chow time, Camden asked Tiny if they could speak. Tiny directed his bodyguards to give them space, and Camden proceeded to tell him the story about the basketball court.

"Yo, Tiny, I need to call in that one favor to help out my one and only son. It's about a little altercation with Big G on the courts in Crystal Cove. I'm sure you know about it 'cause nothing happens on the outside you don't hear about. But my son…I can tell you he didn't know who Big G was. Do you think you can do me that solid?"

Tiny thought about it for a minute, but Camden knew not to rush the situation. Then Tiny said, "You know, I heard about that altercation. Didn't know he was your son. Your son held his own, and my brother, well, he was a disappointment. Your kid got heart. Let me make a few calls and get the story for myself. If the story lines up with what I heard, I'll see what I can do. You know blood is thicker than water, right?" Camden nodded, and they parted ways.

A couple of hours later, Tiny came to Camden's jail cell and stood in the doorway. He stood 6"4' and about 300 pounds and could barely fit through the doorway. Camden stood up to greet him. Tiny said, "Okay, look, I talked to my peeps. Your boy don't need to worry, they won't touch him, but me and you…we even."

Camden nodded his head in agreement. "Thanks, man." He held out his hand, but Tiny instead gave him a salute and walked off.

Feeling relieved that his son would not be harmed, Camden ran to get the approval to use the phone. He called Frankie and told him about the conversation with Tiny.

"That's what's up," said Frankie. "I'll tell Luke if he finds him to let him know the good news, but I think your son ran off."

After being released, Camden's first stop was Ms. Debbie's house to see Karden. It was such a relief to know he didn't have to worry about Big G and his crew.

* * *

Grandma Debbie was still in shock seeing Camden on her porch. She stepped to the side so that he could walk in. He sat on the couch while Grandma sat in her favorite recliner.

Debbie was still looking at him as if seeing a ghost. "You finally got out. I'm still trying to grasp it all."

Camden explained to Grandma Debbie that he was falsely arrested and planned on doing whatever it took to get his conviction overturned, but it was going to take time. He expressed he was sorry for not being there for Karden for all these years, but he did not want Karden seeing him in prison.

"I know I should have at least written, but I was too ashamed." He hung his head, hiding his emotions.

Grandma Debbie said, "Baby, we all make mistakes. The good news is you are here now. Thank God there's still time but..." Her voice trailed off.

Camden said, "What's wrong? Is it Karden?"

"Yes, but it's going to be alright. He ran away with his friend Caniya to get away from some trouble he got in while he was here. Scared me half to death, but he's good. Actually…he's with your brother in New York."

"He's with Richard?!" he asked incredulously. Then he held his head back and laughed. "That's my big brother. Always on the job to protect and serve. I know all about Karden's trouble."

Grandma Debbie raised an eyebrow. "How so?"

"It's a long story. You are just going to have to trust me! I took care of it."

Debbie lifted her hands, "Hallelujah, thank you, Jesus."

Camden asked, "When will they be home?"

"They will be here in a few days. Matter of fact, I'm planning a welcome-home celebration with Caniya's mother. Did you know Caniya is Richard's daughter? Okay, that's another story for another time. But in the meantime, I have an idea!"

She shared her thoughts with him, and he was all in!

Chapter 16

THE JOURNEY BACK HOME

Dream Ford, Kayla Mason, Preston Staten Hall

"Last call for Flight 723 departing New York City to Jacksonville, Florida."

Caniya, Karden, and Richard had depended on an Uber to get them to the airport, which was on time, but the New York traffic was backed up due to a traffic accident, so the three of them had to run like crazy not to miss their flight. Luckily, Richard brought Caniya a new suitcase because the old one was done. As they ran up to the ticket counter, the airline host said, "You made it just in time. We were about to close the doors."

Out of breath, Richard, Caniya, and Karden boarded the plane home. Richard could only get two seats together, so he let Karden and Caniya sit together while he sat in the very last row of the aircraft. This was the first time either of the kids had been on a plane.

They were excited and scared. Caniya asked Karden if she could have the window seat so she could remember her first airplane ride. Karden replied, "Sure, shorty, you can have it." Caniya was all buckled up, ready to go. She paid close attention to the flight attendant as they went over the emergency protocols. She wanted to know what to do just in case the plane went down. Karden just pulled out his phone and started looking at his Instagram page.

The captain greeted everyone on the flight and announced that the flight would be a little over two hours.

"We are going to be in the air for two hours?" Karden asked Caniya.

"I guess so if we want to make it to Florida," she replied.

Caniya leaned over to Karden and asked, "You think we gonna get in trouble when we get back? I mean, they sounded okay on the phone."

Karden smirked. "Duh, yeah, you know we in mad trouble, so prepare yourself to be yelled at and grounded."

Caniya nodded, "Yeah, you right." She pulled out her phone to see if she had any new messages, put her phone on airplane mode, and looked out the window.

Karden and Caniya didn't have much to say to each other on the flight. Karden slept most of the way there while Caniya started jotting down fashion ideas. She pulled out one of the magazines in the backset holder, and to her surprise, it was a *Teen Vogue* magazine. Caniya couldn't contain her excitement. She would go through every inch of that magazine, and before she knew it, the flight attendants were directing everyone to buckle up because they were about to land.

"Wow, we here already?" Caniya asked Karden, but Karden didn't hear her because he was still asleep. Caniya shoved Karden a couple times until he finally woke up. "Dude, we here, wake up." Karden took a big stretch and wiped his eyes. He was also amazed how short the flight seemed.

They gathered their luggage and exited the plane. Richard said, "You can tell when you arrive to Florida because it's super-hot as soon as you get off the plane." Richard had gotten used to the New York weather so much that he had totally forgotten how hot it got in Florida.

Their Uber ride was right on time for the hour ride to Sheila's house. Karden sat in the front with the Uber driver while Richard and Caniya sat in the back.

Karden was excited, but at the same time, he was nervous. Every now and then, his heart would start racing as an internal ball of emotions would collide, and he didn't know how to feel or what to expect. It was rare that his grandmother punished him, and he tried so hard to do everything right. He really did not like disappointing her, yet he was trying to brace himself for the worst! No phone privileges, grounded for days, no b-ball, no video games… all he could picture was a bunch of "no's." Even though on the phone everything sounded like all was forgiven, he knew how adults could be once the shock wore off. He checked his watch for the hundredth time and kept his eyes on the GPS showing their progress to Caniya's house.

He stared out the window, blinking back emotional tears. It was nice to know that he had an uncle, but he felt a slight twinge of jealousy that Caniya, his newly found cousin, was able to reconnect with her dad. He was happy for them, but he wished he had his dad in his life. He sniffled faintly and breathed deeply to collect himself. Then he quickly shifted his thoughts to how lucky they were to be safe, and in the end, it didn't matter what awaited him at home, including his altercation with the Viper Kings. He'd have to come clean and find a way to keep them safe. All in all, he couldn't wait to get there and hug his grandmother.

Caniya was overjoyed at having her dad back. It was like a dream come true. While they rode home, she couldn't help but smile to herself about the chain of events that had taken place in such a short time. Even though she was determined to be on her own and make a name for herself, she found out that her mother really did care about her, and over the phone, it sounded very sincere.

Caniya's smile quickly faded though. Many times, she thought she and her mom were doing well only for them to get into another bad argument, fussing all the time. Caniya glanced out of the window to hide her sadness. Soon, she was noting the familiar sites and landmarks as they got closer to her home. She wondered if things would be better or the same, and if they stayed the same, what would she do. Was this a mistake coming back home? She wanted to believe that everything would be just fine. If nothing else, she had found her dad, and that was like a piece of heaven.

Sensing Caniya's mood shift, Richard grabbed Caniya's hand and said, "Everything is going to be okay, Baby Bear. I'm right here with you."

Chapter 17

REUNITED

Camille Carmichael, Dream Ford, Kayla Mason, Kendall Jackson, Preston Staten Hall

Sheila had been shopping, excited that in two hours, her baby Caniya would be home safe. Everyone was now at the house, including Grandma Debbie, helping to get the decorations up and food prepared for the celebration. Two hours flew by, because before they knew it, they heard a car in the driveway.

Upon reaching the house, Richard jumped out, while Caniya and Karden moved without urgency. Richard leaned into the car. "Let's go, kids. Get on out."

Together, Karden and Caniya exited the car, both lost in their own thoughts wondering what waited for them behind the closed door to Caniya's house. Both looked at each other and then embraced. Caniya whispered in his ear, "No matter what, I got you."

Karden replied, "Me too, cousin."

They separated, and Richard walked over to them. "Why y'all look so worried? Trust me, it's going to be okay."

Karden and Caniya nodded, neither knowing that the other had knots in their stomachs and fear in their hearts.

Richard rang the bell and knocked. "It's open," Sheila yelled, and as they walked in the door, everyone shouted and applauded, "Welcome home!"

Caniya and Karden were shocked to see all their family and friends together. Sheila ran up to Caniya and gave her a big hug, squeezing her tight. "I'm so sorry for everything I've put you through. I wasn't acting like a mother. Everything will be different from now on."

Caniya smiled and hugged her mother back, both shedding a few tears. Caniya's siblings were now joining in the group hug.

Karden looked around the room and saw Grandma Debbie. He could see her wiping tears from her eyes. Karden made his way through the small gathering to Grandma Debbie and hugged her so tightly.

"Karden, I missed you so much. Please don't ever leave me like that again."

Karden replied, "I'm sorry for not calling to let you know I was okay. I promise not to scare you like this ever again." They continued to embrace each other for a while.

Sheila looked around the room and saw that everyone was crying and laughing, full of joy.

Sheila knew there was one more thing she had to do. She knew she had to apologize and make things right with Richard. Sheila walked over to Richard and asked, "Can we talk?" She pulled him to the side.

"Richard, I am so sorry for the way I acted over the years we were together. You didn't deserve it, and I really want you to know how very sorry I am. I now realize that I was taking my childhood hurt and pain out on you and Caniya, and I'm so deeply sorry for that. I'm going to go to therapy to work through my pain so that I can be a better mother to my children. Thank you for bringing them home. This means the world to me what you've done."

Richard gave Sheila a hug, showing he appreciated her apology.

There was another knock on the door. Grandma Debbie said to Karden, "It's for you."

Karden thought it was strange but said, "Okay," and walked to open it, a bit unsure.

Everyone was looking to see who could be at the door, and when Karden opened the door, there Camden stood. Grandma Debbie made her way to the door and pulled Camden inside while Karden just stood there in awe.

Sheila yelled out, "Camden, is that you? Sheila gave him a big hug and said, "Welcome to the family."

Richard was in the kitchen talking with Kirk when he heard Sheila yelling for him. When he turned the corner, he saw his brother, Camden, standing there with a smile on his face. The two of them made eye contact and walked towards each other. Once face to face, they embraced each other. Richard loved his baby brother and had always felt guilty that he couldn't help with getting him out of prison.

Karden stood near his grandmother in disbelief that his father was right in front of him.

Camden turned his attention to Karden. He was amazed at how much he had grown and how much he resembled his mother. The room became quiet. You could have heard a pin drop.

Camden said, "Son."

Karden replied, "Dad?"

Camden grabbed Karden and pulled him in close. "I'm so sorry, Karden. I'm sorry I wasn't there for you after your mom passed. Please forgive me."

Karden didn't respond. He just held on to his father. There wasn't a dry eye in the room.

The party was like a reunion. Sheila, Kirk, Isis, and Cole were reunited with Caniya. Grandma Debbie and Camden were reunited with Karden, and Richard got some closure with Sheila. It was a day that none of them would forget.

After the party ended, Grandma Debbie and Camden took Karden home. Camden and Karden would stay up all night talking and looking at photos. Karden had many stories to tell his father about his basketball skills and all the trophies he had won.

Richard's flight was scheduled for the following day, but he called to extend his leave so that he could spend more time with Caniya and his brother. Richard grabbed a hotel for a few nights, and before he fell off to sleep, he vowed to do whatever he could to help his family. Number one on the list was regular visits with Caniya.

Back at Caniya's house, everyone had gone to bed except for Sheila and Caniya.

Sheila said, "Well, it's just the two of us now. Tomorrow, I have a lot to tell you, but tonight, how about I fix some popcorn and we watch a movie together? You down with that?"

Caniya smiled, "Yes mom, I would love to. But I pick the movie."

Sheila agreed. "Deal!" They stayed up all night watching movies, bonding, and laughing. Caniya was happier than she could ever remember.

ABOUT THE AUTHORS

Camille Carmichael is thirteen years old and loves to play softball and basketball. She enjoys spending time outdoors and performing with the dance ministry at her church. Camille wants to go to college to become a dermatologist and an aesthetician.

Dream Ford is a fourteen-year-old eighth grade student who enjoys school and family. To succeed, Dream believes she must aspire to learn and experience as many things as possible. In addition, Dream is a comedian at heart. She loves to laugh and entertain her family and friends with funny pranks and skits. She also loves modeling and always gives her best to whatever she does.

Kayla Mason is a tenth grader who enjoys cooking. She aspires to become a chef or attend John Jay University after graduating high school. She loves to swim, and her favorite sport is volleyball. Besides becoming an author this year, Kayla plans to write a stage play.

Kendall Jackson was born in October 2006. Kendall is in the eleventh grade. She is an exemplary student who excels in her classes. Kendall is enrolled in the foundation of health program where she will become a certified pharmacy technician when she graduates from the twelfth grade. Kendall has a passion for writing and photography. She loves to capture special moments on camera of her family and friends. She also loves to write poetry. Kendall is very friendly, loves to work, and is loved by everyone she meets. Kendall is also involved in her church where she participates in the dance ministry and stage performances.

Preston S. Hall is twelve years old and resides in Baltimore, Maryland. Preston started his own Juneteenth business at nine years old. He is fluent in English and Chinese and is currently learning three more languages. Preston has participated in many robotics competitions and has assisted in coding for his school computer science club. He enjoys learning MMA, photography, and basketball.

CONNECT WITH US!

Email: info@youthwritersrock.com

Website: www.youthwritersrock.com

Facebook: /youthwritersrock

Instagram: @youthwriterschallenge